IN TIME OF WAR

A Selection of Recent Titles by Nicola Thorne

* *available from Severn House*

IN TIME OF WAR

Nicola Thorne

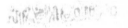

This first world edition published in Great Britain 2000 by
SEVERN HOUSE PUBLISHERS LTD of
9–15 High Street, Sutton, Surrey SM1 1DF.
This first world edition published in the USA 2000 by
SEVERN HOUSE PUBLISHERS INC of
595 Madison Avenue, New York, N.Y. 10022.

British Library Cataloguing in Publication Data

Thorne, Nicola
    In time of war. - (People of this Parish saga ; bk. 6)
    1.   World War,   1939-1945 - Fiction
    I.   Title
    823.9'14 [F]

    ISBN 0-7278-5552-2

Typeset by Palimpsest Book Production Ltd.,
Polmont, Stirlingshire, Scotland.
Printed and bound in Great Britain by
MPG Books Ltd, Bodmin, Cornwall.

CONTENTS

The Woodville Family 1800–1939

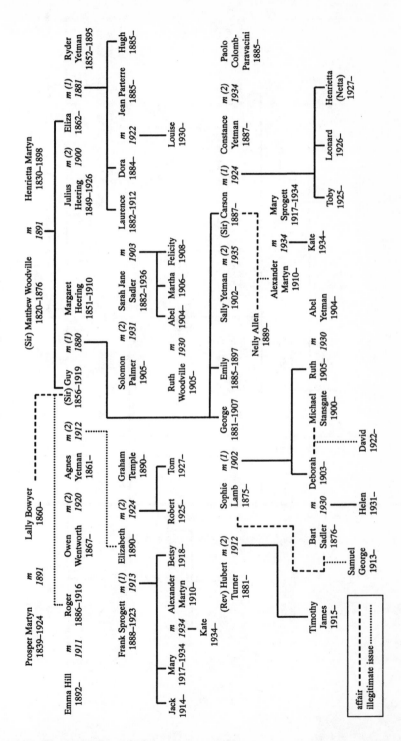

The Yetman Family 1800–1939

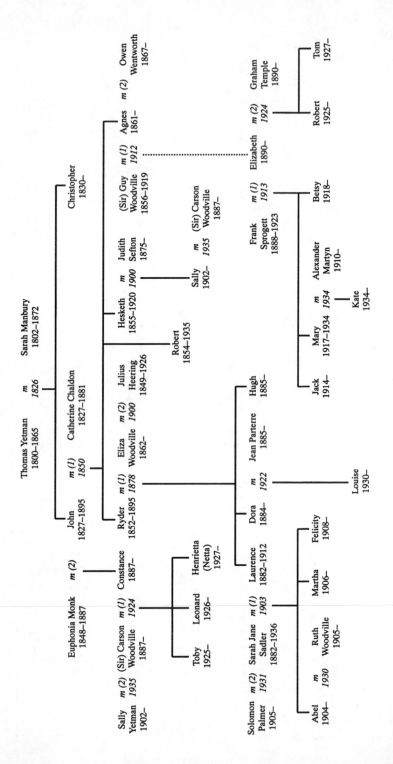

The *People of This Parish* Series

The Story So Far

In 1880 young Sir Guy Woodville brings his new Dutch bride, Margaret, to his ancient Dorset family home, Pelham's Oak. With Margaret comes a much-needed dowry to restore the fortunes of the impoverished but noble Woodville family. Guy has a rebellious, high-spirited younger sister, Eliza, who spurns her family's attempts to marry her well. She elopes with Ryder Yetman, the son of a local builder, causing great scandal in the sleepy market town of Wenham over which the Woodvilles have presided for centuries. Margaret and Guy have three children: pious George, who elopes with the rector's daughter, Sophie, to Papua New Guinea where he dies of fever; an only daughter, Emily, who dies young; and the heir, Carson, a charming rebel with an eye for the ladies who would rather be a farmer than a baronet.

Eliza, meanwhile, has been happily married to Ryder, who becomes a prosperous builder. They too have three children. When Ryder is killed in an accident, Eliza marries the brother of Margaret, her sister-in-law – a cold, mean man, who refuses to help his stepson Laurence when he is facing bankruptcy. Laurence commits suicide, leaving an embittered widow, Sarah-Jane, and a young family.

Years later, Sophie Woodville returns as a widow to her birthplace, with two young children. She is welcomed neither by George's parents, who feel she is responsible for his untimely death, nor by her own, who also disapproved of the marriage. Sophie endures many vicissitudes before marrying her father's curate, despite knowing that she is carrying the child of another man.

Carson, after his mother's death, is prevailed upon to propose to a wealthy young girl, Connie, in order to save Pelham's Oak and the Woodvilles from financial ruin. But he does not love her, and when his father remarries, to the supposedly rich Agnes, Connie leaves Wenham to travel the world with her wealthy guardian.

Carson then inherits the title from his dead father, and returns a hero at the end of the First World War, only to find the Woodville estate once more in financial difficulties due largely to the excesses of Agnes, his stepmother.

Soon after Carson's return the rejected Connie, now transformed from a duckling into a swan, once more enters his life. His stepmother, however, contines to plague him, especially after her marriage to a fortune-hunter called Owen Wentworth, who assumes a spurious title and marries Agnes for her money only to find that she has none. He makes off with what jewellery she possesses and she is left destitute, dependent on Carson and Connie.

Meanwhile, Agnes's daughter by Sir Guy, Elizabeth, lives in penury with her war-wounded husband and three children, only to discover that she is a Woodville by birth. She is determined to exact revenge on the family who disowned her, but kind-hearted Carson tries to make amends.

A decade later, Bart Sadler, the former lover of Sophie Turner who left many years before to seek his fortune overseas, returns to Wenham a rich man and makes a conquest of Sophie's discontented daughter Deborah.

Sarah-Jane Yetman, for many years a widow, falls prey to the charms of a much younger man and, to her family's disapproval, runs away with him.

Dora Yetman, trapped in a platonic marriage to Frenchman Jean, renews her relationship with her one-time lover May Williams and goes away with her, but is eventually reunited with her husband.

Meanwhile Sir Carson Woodville after many years of apparently happy marriage to Connie, which have brought him three children, is caught up with the love of his youth, Nelly, the mother of his son Alexander, and risks everything.

Alexander by now is a personable, very wealthy young man who, against the wishes of the family, falls in love with his cousin Mary Sprogett, who is only seventeen. They elope and Mary subsequently dies in childbirth leaving Alexander with a daughter, Kate, and very bitter about the fact that his family hid from him the truth about his birth for so long.

Connie and Carson have divorced and both remarry. Meanwhile, war is approaching and Alexander seeks the help of Bart Sadler, who has extensive business connections abroad, to help rescue Reuben Schwartz, a Jewish art dealer from Germany. Alexander then finds himself falling in love with Reuben's beautiful daughter, Irene.

Part One

The Darkest Days

1939–1944

One

In the eyes of many people it was an inauspicious time for a wedding: Hitler had overrun Czechoslovakia; Chamberlain had guaranteed the help of the English nation to Poland should the same thing happen to them, and he had introduced conscription. For the two people in love it was a time of extremes: great personal happiness combined with high anxiety.

Britain was clearly preparing for war, and village halls up and down the land were seething with people anxious, should it be required, to do their bit. The ARP was taking volunteers, the ranks of the WVS bursting with new recruits, while men young and old were eager to enlist in the armed forces.

There was an all-pervasive spirit of comradeship that seemed to give zest to the nation and engender an atmosphere that was almost festive.

But the wedding reception held that day at Pelham's Oak, near the small Dorset market town of Wenham, was low-key in comparison to others which the older members of the Woodville family could recall. Usually there had been a white wedding at Wenham Parish Church followed by a huge reception at the house, to which family friends and estate workers were all invited, and the celebrations seemed to go on for days.

But on this occasion instead of making their vows in church Alexander Martyn and Irene Schwartz had been

5

married at a registry office in London and the following day there was a luncheon party at the Dorset home of Alexander's father Carson. Close relations were there, a handful of friends and the bride's parents, Reuben and Alma Schwartz.

The undoubted guest of honour was Bart Sadler who, the previous year, had helped to spirit Reuben from the Nazi concentration camp of Sachenhausen.

Bart had not always been in favour with the Woodville family but now it was time to let bygones be bygones, especially with Eliza, Alexander's aunt, who found herself placed next to him at table. Bart had with him his son Sam, who was helping him to run his business while Bart continued his mysterious trips abroad exchanging goods for human cargo: Jewish victims of Nazi persecution.

Conversation was difficult, Eliza was annoyed at the place setting, but good manners prevented her from complaining.

"Did you go to the wedding Mrs Heering?" Bart enquired politely making another attempt at conversation.

Eliza shook her head.

"Only Carson and Lally and the Schwartzes were there. They wanted to keep it quiet."

Eliza paused, conscious of the restraint between them, and her expression changed. "I wanted to tell you, frankly, Mr Sadler, that what you did in Germany was very commendable. I admire you."

"Thank you Mrs Heering." Bart attempted a modest smile. "I assure you there was no personal bravery involved. It was a matter of manipulating people, using my business connections. I also made a small profit on the side – not from Mr Schwartz – but I always travel to Germany with a full load. I didn't even meet Mr Schwartz until he was safely over the border." Bart inclined his head towards Eliza. "But I must tell you that almost of equal importance to me at this moment is the renewal of our acquaintanceship. The hope that this means you will forgive me for the past."

Eliza stiffened.

"What happened over the business of my house happened

a long time ago. As these things sometimes turn out it was for the best. I am not only very happy at Riversmead I think I prefer it to Upper Park, which you bought from me behind my back."

"I still detect a note of bitterness, Mrs Heering," Bart said contritely. "I can't tell you how sorry I am. I behaved in a very stupid and clumsy fashion when I came back from abroad all those years ago. I have learned my lesson since."

Eliza thought it was difficult to sense any real sorrow on that self-satisfied mask that was the face of Bart Sadler. He had always been trouble in the neighbourhood, causing it before he left and again when he returned. It was too easy to misinterpret his motives, but he had made nothing but mischief to her family.

She was relieved when Bart turned away to talk to his son Sam who, despite a rather bullish, self-confident appearance had nothing to say, perhaps out of shyness in front of relatives he had had little to do with before. His mother, Sophie Turner, had once been married to Eliza's nephew George. Sam was a tall, saturnine young man who very much resembled his father.

Momentarily, Eliza had the opportunity to look round at the members of the family gathered at the table. It put her in a nostalgic mood as she thought back over the years recalling, as a woman of seventy-seven and a matriarch must, all the occasions, joyful and tragic, connected with the family home of Pelham's Oak where she had been born.

Next to her was the head of the family Carson, fourteenth baronet, engaged in conversation with Alma Schwartz. Alexander and Irene sat together in the middle and, also locked in conversation with their neighbours, were Lally, Alexander's adoptive mother, Carson's wife Sally, Eliza's daughter Dora and her husband Jean Parterre who had only just arrived that day from France.

With a few taps on a glass to call for silence, Carson rose glancing at the happy faces of Alexander and Irene raised expectantly towards him.

7

"I won't talk for long," he said, "but I did want to tell you how full my heart is on this day to know that Alexander has again found a happiness he so deserves. We live in troubled times but life goes on, renewing itself. It is in the hands of young people like Alexander and Irene that our future lies." He raised his glass. "To Alexander and Irene."

"Alexander and Irene, Alexander and Irene," murmured the guests.

As they sat down again Alexander rose and slowly gazed around him as if committing to memory every face there before speaking.

"Thank you, Father. It is, needless to say, a very happy day for Irene and me. It is wonderful to be reunited with the family here at Pelham's Oak and to have you all with us, especially Reuben and Alma." He glanced towards his parents-in-law. "In this connection, I have to express my heartfelt thanks to Bart Sadler for restoring Reuben to us." He raised his glass. "This is for you, Bart, for all you've done . . . and may your good work continue," as Bart smiled his thanks Alexander lowered his voice, "because I think it will be necessary. I fear that dark times lie ahead, but let the thought not spoil our day. Irene and I raise our glasses to our friends and families. Long may we all live in peace and harmony with one another, and may the nations of the world succeed in achieving peace and harmony among themselves too."

"Peace and harmony," everyone murmured fervently, but there were doubts in many voices that it would come true.

After lunch they gathered in the white and gold drawing room which had seen so many grand receptions in the past.

"Do you worry about a war, Jean?" Eliza asked her son-in-law who, coffee cup in hand, had joined her.

"Everyone worries about a war; but I think it is inevitable now. I have thought so for a long time. I worry about my vines." He frowned and put his cup to his lips.

"He's always worrying about his vines," Dora said a little

shrilly as she joined them. "The most important things in his life."

"That is not true, my love," Jean said in the tired tone of voice of one who has had to say the same thing over and over again. "You and our daughter are the most important things in my life."

Eliza looked round. "Where are the children? I thought they might join us."

"Oh, they're playing happily. Unfortunately it's a game of war." Carson, hearing the end of the conversation, had now joined them. "I dare say at their age I would have done the same. We thought formal lunch with the family would be too boring for them." Carson's sons Toby and Leonard were home from school for the summer holiday. Their mother Connie, from whom Carson was divorced, lived with her second husband in Venice. Remaining with her was Netta her youngest child and only daughter. Usually Toby and Leonard went to Venice for the holidays, but because of the international situation they were staying in England and their sister would soon join them.

As if on cue the children, washed and neatly dressed, were ushered in by a smiling nursemaid. With Toby and Leonard were Louise, Dora's daughter, and Alexander's five-year-old daughter Kate whose mother, Mary, had died giving birth to her. The girls, in pretty dresses, hair well brushed, appeared in awe both of the grown-ups and the two older boys to whom, in the war game, they had been hostages. It was rather a relief to get away.

The rough and tumble of children's play was alien to both the girls, especially Kate in the over-protective atmosphere in which she was being brought up.

Kate looked relieved to see her father and ran over to him, hiding her head against his leg.

"My darling," he said tenderly, "did you have a nice game?"

Kate shook her head.

"I want *you*, Daddy."

"Daddy wants you too." Alexander led her over to a chair and sat down. "And when Irene and I come back from our honeymoon we shall all be together."

Kate looked at him, eyes shining. She was an incredibly beautiful child with golden hair, peach-blossom skin and cornflower-blue eyes. She was also rather spoiled, with her own devoted nurse Massie, her doting grandmother Lally and her adoring father racked by guilt because he felt he had let her young mother die.

Kate had decided that Irene intruded in this pleasant scheme of things and tried to ignore her whenever she could. In fact, she wished that she would go away, but now it appeared she was to be around forever.

"For always?" Kate insisted.

"For always. Well . . ." But he stopped. What was the purpose of mentioning something which the child would not understand and which in any case might not ever happen? The War.

The children now occupied the attention of the grown-ups who broke into small groups. Outside it was raining, inside a great fire roared in the chimney. Tea was eventually served after which it was time for the bridal pair to leave on their honeymoon.

Everyone drifted to the hall and on to the porch, the late afternoon sun struggled to appear through thick grey clouds. They stood around in groups chatting, laughing, smoking until Irene appeared, hatless, carrying a white linen coat, to match the dress she'd changed into, over her arm. She favoured white; it contrasted so well with her dark good looks. She was raven-haired and high-cheekboned, with brown almost tawny-coloured eyes. She always wore a lot of make-up and, usually, scarlet lipstick. She was tall and slim, flamboyant, sophisticated, the very antithesis to the petite, shy and ethereally beautiful Mary who had died so tragically at the age of seventeen.

Following her came Alexander, his arm still round his daughter who clung to him. Alexander too was possessed of striking good looks being dark like his wife with short black hair, brushed back from his forehead, deeply recessed eyes that seemed black, and high, distinctive cheekbones that gave him a slightly Slav look. He wore a grey pinstriped suit and carried a trilby in his hand. After smothering Kate with kisses he delivered her to the care of Massie and Lally who looked at her anxiously fearing an outburst.

The newly married couple then passed through the crowd gathered on the porch where there were more kisses, hugs, promises to write, to take care. Toby and Leonard on their best behaviour stood on either side of their father and stepmother. Little Kate had to be restrained by Lally and Massie from trying to join her father and, as Lally had feared, collapsed into tears.

Looking up Alexander was immediately distressed and, leaving his bride, hurried back up the steps to kiss Kate again and repeat his reassurances. Now Lally looked on the verge of tears. She hadn't wanted them to go abroad.

There was an air of general pandemonium. Irene, looking tense, hugged her fur round her as she leaned against the car waiting for Alexander, a cigarette between her fingers. Kate was finally reassured, promised extravagant presents and the swift return of her father. Alexander rushed back to join his bride, kissed her cheek and tenderly ushered her into the car.

At the back of the crowd Bart Sadler stood, detached from the proceedings, his son beside him, smoking a cigarette and watching events. Suddenly Irene, about to get into the car, saw him and rushed up the steps towards him, flinging her arms around him and whispering: "Thank you again." Then she turned and, as if she too like Kate was reluctant to leave the reassuring parental presence, embraced her mother and father who wore brave smiles. After all worse things had happened to them in the last few years than losing their daughter to a *goy*, and hadn't Reuben been rescued by one?

Then Irene ran down the steps to join her smiling husband

11

who once again helped her into the car. Waving towards the porch he eased himself into the driving seat and the car roared into life.

An arm fluttered from either side as it sped down the drive, through the double row of plane trees, out of sight.

Eliza, clutching Louise firmly by the hand, waved, as did the rest of the family until the car disappeared. But instead of a happy smile, her expression was one of anxiety at the thought of the uncertain future ahead, not only for the newly married couple, but for all those present, especially the young.

Irene and Alexander sat close together on the balcony of the villa, hands linked. In front of them a great swathe of moonlight seemed to cut the water of the lake in two, one side dark, the other light, like day and night. Around them towered the mountains, an unseen but almost palpable presence. It was true there were soldiers in the town of Como but no other signs of warlike preparation, and the soldiers had a festive air as though they were on holiday. Despite the fact that Italy and Germany had signed a pact of steel pledging a military alliance it was all extraordinarily peaceful.

On a table next to them was a bottle of wine in an ice bucket, two tall glasses half full of amber-coloured liquid. Irene wore a long white dress simply cut with a deep V neckline, white sandals on her feet and a broad gold choker round her neck. Her fingers were adorned with heavy, ornate antique rings set with large stones beside which her wedding ring and even her ruby and diamond engagement ring seemed insignificant.

They were in Alexander's villa by the side of Lake Como, a place he had bought as a retreat from the pressures of his busy life. By day they walked in the mountains or lay basking in the sun on the terrace, and Irene's tanned body radiated health. Her make-up, her orange-coloured lipstick blended perfectly with her tan and her gleaming dark curls.

Alexander thought he was more in love with her every

day and not only with her beauty but with her sweetness of disposition, the nobility of her character, her generosity of nature. He leaned forward to pour more wine into their glasses and, as he sat back, his lips caressed her cheek and she eagerly turned her mouth to him in response.

"Something like this should never end," he murmured.

"I think I could stay here for ever," Irene replied. "Only we can't, can we?"

"Unfortunately, no."

"Did she love it too?"

"She?" Alexander turned to her enquiringly.

"Mary."

"Yes. I bought the villa for her as a wedding present. Only she never saw it again."

"It must have been dreadful for you."

"It was. Dreadful." He sighed heavily.

"I remember her very well. She was so terribly pretty, like a doll." As Alexander continued to gaze broodingly over the water, Irene went on, "Does talking about her upset you?"

He turned to her reassuringly. "Not at all. I don't think we should forget her, but you must remember that now you're my wife and I love you. My love for Mary is locked away, maybe in the grave with her. I mourned her, but I don't think that means I don't deserve another life."

"Of course it doesn't." She clasped his hand. "If it upsets you to be here . . ."

"No. It doesn't. It is a happy place. Father and Sally became engaged here, made love here for the first time I believe. *It* is happy and peaceful, but how long it will remain so . . ." He paused. "But let's not talk about the war."

"There may not be one."

"No one seems to be trying very hard to stop it."

"Darling . . ."

"Yes?"

"*If* there is a war, if it is declared, what will you do?"

"I haven't thought about it. Join up, I suppose. I expect my call-up papers any day."

13

"The army?"

"No. The air force as I love flying." His hand closed over hers. "Darling, don't spoil this lovely evening. Drink up and we'll go and have some dinner."

Every night they ate at a different restaurant usually within walking distance of the villa. Then they strolled back and, after a final nightcap on the terrace, went to bed.

This night was like the others that had gone before except that to Alexander Irene seemed preoccupied, not her usual sparkling self. He wondered if the talk before dinner on the terrace had upset her. Or if it was because it was officially the last night of their honeymoon. The next day they were due to go to Venice to fetch Netta and return with her to England.

"It seems as though you haven't enjoyed the evening, darling," he said handing her a brandy once they were back on the terrace.

"Oh no!" Startled she looked up. "It's been *wonderful*. Every evening, every moment with you is wonderful."

"Was it the talk about Mary – or the war?"

"I am worried about the prospect of war, Alexander." Carefully she put down her glass without touching the contents, then groped in her bag for a cigarette which Alexander darted forward to light. Then he lit one for himself and sat down beside her.

"What makes you bring it up now?" He looked perplexed. "I feel further away from the war here than I do at home. In fact I never thought about it until tonight."

"I think about it all the time . . . my friends in Germany. Alexander, I have a particular friend, Stella Schapira, who still lives in Berlin. We were at art school together and shared an apartment. I am somehow very anxious about Stella. I can't get her out of my mind."

"When we get back I'll ask Bart—"

"No, Alexander." Her hand rested on his arm. "I want to go myself to Stella to try and persuade her of the danger and to leave Berlin. I worry about her and Ernst her boyfriend."

"Perhaps she has left already?"

"Oh, I'm sure she hasn't or she would have contacted me."

Suddenly the night which had been so wonderful, so full of promise seemed fraught with anxiety and fear.

"Irene you can't possibly go yourself," Alexander exploded. "I forbid it."

"But you can't *forbid* it Alexander." A steely note entered her voice. "Even though I am your wife I have rights, you know."

"I am perfectly aware of that but you forget how much I love you, how frantic I would be if anything happened to you."

"Nothing will happen to me," she said firmly. "I am married to an Englishman. I have a British passport. My name is Martyn not Schwartz. You don't think there are any English people in Berlin? There are *plenty* of English people in Berlin. We are not at war, you know. I will slip in and out, hopefully to return with Stella."

"But what if she is already in a concentration camp?"

"She is not. I heard from her not so long ago. She sounded happy. Her boyfriend isn't Jewish and she feels safe. She doesn't want to leave him."

"Then let him take care of her."

"Alexander, I don't know how you can be so cruel."

"Darling, I am *not* cruel; but the thought of you going to Berlin terrifies me."

"Well it doesn't terrify me," she said firmly. "I can slip over there and be back before you know I've gone, especially from Italy since Mussolini and Hitler are such friends."

"I forbid it," Alexander said, and his mouth closed in a thin stubborn line. "If necessary I'll prevent you by force."

That night for the first time on their honeymoon they didn't make love but kept to their own sides of the bed.

Connie said, "I'm so sorry we missed the wedding. Paolo hasn't been well." She looked anxiously over at her husband who sat upright in his chair and obligingly coughed as if to confirm what she'd said.

"You worry too much, my darling. Have some more of this veal, Irene. It is very good."

"It *is* very good," smiling, Irene shook her head, "but no more, thanks." She looked pale and tired after two sleepless nights, the result of the first serious disagreement she and Alexander had had since they had known each other. She knew his reaction had been inspired by fear, by love, but still it showed a new and authoritative side of him that worried her.

They had arrived the previous day in Venice to pick up Netta and take her home with them, the honeymoon now at an end.

Connie had married Count Colomb-Paravacini in 1934 following her divorce from Carson. She was fifty-two and he was seventeen years her senior but had long adored her, even before her marriage to Carson, and when it had broken up he was there by her side like a faithful old dog. In appearance he resembled a typical English gentleman: tall, with twinkly eyes, a noble bald dome with a white fringe, and a white moustache.

The Palazzo Colomb-Paravacini on its fourteenth-century foundations overlooked the Grand Canal in a position of unparallelled magnificence. They sat now in the grand dining room with strong thick stone walls, built to keep out the enemy and perhaps also the winter chill, hung with fabulous tapestries. The mullioned windows provided a wonderful view of the ancient city across the Canal.

Netta had greeted her half-brother with wild excitement and kept wriggling in her chair interrupting the conversation of the grown-ups.

"Anyone would think you were glad to leave me," her mother said with a rueful smile. Connie had the look of the well-bred, quintessential English woman. She was tall and slim, small breasted, her brown hair streaked with grey, fine lines round her mouth and eyes. She had never been a beauty but had aged gracefully and well. She wore gold-framed spectacles which gave her a rather stern, studious air.

"She wants to see her brothers again," Paolo said tactfully. "We shall miss her."

"Will Netta be coming back?" Alexander asked.

"Of course." Paolo looked surprised. "I hope the boys too will be here for the rest of the summer. Why should they not be?"

"Well," Alexander cleared his throat, "the international situation . . ."

"Oh, you're talking of war." Paolo leaned back in his chair and thoughtfully tapped the table with his fingers. "Frankly I don't think there will be one. The powers will come to their senses. Mussolini is a strong influence on Hitler and he is a good man."

"Mussolini is a *good* man?" Irene exclaimed putting down her knife and fork. "After what happened in Abyssinia?"

"I am not talking about Abyssinia which, maybe, was regrettable – though we undoubtedly did have a claim to it, but he has done a lot for Italy, built magnificent new roads, railway stations."

"I don't know how you can endorse his Fascist views." Irene's fine dark eyes gleamed dangerously, and Alexander became concerned on her behalf.

"My dear," Paolo gave a benign smile, "Italian Fascism is not like German Fascism. Mussolini is the best thing to have happened to this country in many years. He has introduced stability and re-established national pride. I am a monarchist, of course, but I have it on good authority that Mussolini and the King get on well. Did he not make Vittorio Emmanuel Emperor of Ethiopia?"

"Perhaps we shouldn't discuss politics." Connie grew increasingly uneasy as the conversation progressed and hurriedly rang a little bell to summon the maid to serve the cheese. "I don't want your time here to be spoilt by misunderstandings. Now, this afternoon – are we going to explore?"

"Oh, yes please," Irene said. "It is my first visit to Venice."

"But not the last, I hope," Paolo said amiably. "You must understand, my dear, that Italy has had a very unhappy history of late and, but for Mussolini, it would have shared the fate of Russia and been overtaken by the communists."

"But what of the Jews?"

"Oh, Mussolini would never harm the Jews. Italian Jews have nothing to fear from him."

After lunch Paolo stayed at home while Connie took Irene and Alexander on a tour of Venice beginning with a trip in the family gondola moored in front of the palazzo and operated by a stalwart member of the staff.

Connie and Irene leaned back, straw hats shielding their faces from the sun. Alexander sat forward with Netta who couldn't contain her excitement that they were to leave the following day for England in Alexander's car which had been left on the mainland.

Irene still felt tense from the conversation at lunch, and she feared she was becoming increasingly isolated from this family into which she had married, not in haste it was true, but perhaps she hadn't found out enough about them, or the man who was now her husband. She and Connie stuck to non-controversial subjects; Connie was anxious to hear news of home, and Irene suspected that she was missing England. Connie wore a plain cotton frock, low-heeled sandals and one had the feeling that fashion was not her prime preoccupation. Irene had no difficulty seeing her, when married to Carson, as a sensible, practical country-woman, pillar of the local community rather than as the wife of an elderly, aristocratic Italian with an admiration of Mussolini.

"Do you really think you will stay here if there is a war?" she asked.

"Oh, undoubtedly." Connie seemed surprised by the question. "We have nothing to fear. I think Carson worries too much. The boys will be perfectly safe here and I shall insist they return."

"I don't think he'll let you." Alexander caught the end of the conversation and moved towards them in the boat.

"Carson will have to let me," Connie said firmly. "We have a legal agreement about the children. It was part of the divorce settlement."

"Do you share Paolo's view?" Alexander asked quietly. "I mean about Mussolini. You were very quiet at lunch."

Connie let a hand fall into the water as the gondola drew in towards St Mark's Square, the boatman looking for a place to anchor and unload his passengers. Finally she said, "I *do* think Mussolini has done a lot of good. He has changed the whole structure of the country, improved the legal and educational systems, remodelled the army. You've no idea what the Italians are like! He needed dictatorial powers to control them. I don't, personally, take to Signor Mussolini and his morals are very suspect. As an Englishwoman I disapprove of dictators but, yes, I do rather agree with Paolo and I do think Hitler's Fascism is not like ours. I don't like *him* at all. He is a thoroughly nasty little man."

"You know Irene is Jewish? She found what Paolo said rather offensive."

Connie nodded. "Yes I do know. We both do. Paolo is too much of a gentleman to wish to offend a guest. He thinks, we both think, that much of what is said about Germany is exaggerated, you know, about the treatment of the Jews, and we feel that everything will be done, *should* be done, by all the parties involved to prevent war."

Connie pulled her hat more firmly over her forehead and turned her gaze to the bank as though to say that that was the end of the matter.

They alighted from the gondola and strolled in the sunshine round the square filled with tourists and flocks of hopeful, fluttering pigeons.

They had tea in Florians and then Alexander and Irene

19

went to look around St Mark's while Connie took Netta to do some shopping.

Dinner that night was eaten at nearby restaurant. Netta had stayed at home because it was intended that an early start should be made. Paolo went out of his way to be charming and even apologised to Irene if he had in any way offended her, assuring her that he had many Jewish friends in Venice and no one could *possibly* call him anti-Semitic.

But still Alexander was glad when dinner ended. He would, on the whole, be relieved when their visit to Venice, indeed to Italy, was over. Most of the honeymoon had been wonderful but the last few days had not been a success, and he could see that Irene had withdrawn into a kind of shell, had become uncharacteristically uncommunicative and distant.

He longed to get back to England, to reassure her of his love and to restore the very real sense of camaraderie that existed between them again.

The window of their bedroom overlooked the canal and when Alexander joined Irene, who had gone up before him, he found her leaning over the sill gazing across to the magically lit city on the other side. She wore a cream silk nightgown that reached to the floor.

"It really is incredibly beautiful," she said turning to him.

But to Alexander the beauty was beside him, not outside, and, detecting a change in her mood, he put his arm tenderly around her.

"Sorry," he said.

"Sorry for what?" She leaned against him.

"It's been a bit of a fiasco. Sorry for the other night. I promise never again to come on with the heavy husband act."

"Then you will not try and stop me going to Berlin?"

He pressed her closer. "My darling I don't advise it. I will, at the very least, try and dissuade you. Look, this is the last night of our honeymoon. Let's drop the subject shall we?"

"If you wish, Alexander." He felt her draw involuntarily away from him.

"I'm surprised at Connie's views," he said in an attempt at appeasement. "About Mussolini. She is being swayed by her husband."

"They say a lot of upper-class English people support the Fascists. Look at Mosley. They supported Franco too."

"It's simply because they feel threatened by communism; but I assure you my family are not pro-Fascist." He gently drew aside her gown and kissed her bare white shoulder. "In this most romantic of all cities let's make love," he murmured.

Alexander woke, aware of strong shafts of sunshine through the shutters. He groped for his watch and saw that it was already eight o'clock. He leaned upon his elbow and rubbed his face, looking to the place beside him for Irene.

But she was already up. He got out of bed and threw back the shutters. It was a beautiful day for their drive. They should reach the frontier by tomorrow evening. He felt refreshed and invigorated despite the fact that he had had little sleep – he and his bride making up for lost time. He called to her, thinking she might be in the bathroom, but there was no reply.

Alexander quickly showered, shaved and dressed. Then he went down the stairs two at a time to the large and gracious hall where a servant stood watching him with a smile.

"The Count and Countess are hoping you will join them for breakfast on the terrace, Mr Martyn," the servant said in good English.

"Thank you," Alexander replied. "Is my wife with them?"

"Ah!" The servant turned to the hall table on which there was a white envelope. "I believe this is for you, sir."

Alexander took the envelope, saw his name written in Irene's bold hand and hurriedly tore it open.

My darling,

    Wasn't it a wonderful night? I will see you when I get back from Berlin, very soon, and we will have many many more like it. Don't worry about me because you know I am yours.

At the bottom was her almost illegible scrawl: Always, Irene.

Alexander went on to the terrace and slumped in a chair while Connie and Paolo looked at him with unfeigned curiosity.

"Something wrong?" Connie enquired raising her eyebrows.

"I've been such a fool," Alexander said striking the table. "Such a terrible, terrible fool."

Two

August 1939

"Any news?"

Alexander, who had been looking out of the window into the square, turned at the sound of Lally's voice and shook his head.

As she came over to him, that special, beautiful fragrance wafted from her reminding him so vividly of his childhood. It was hard to think that Lally, eternally young, eternally beautiful, was now nearly eighty. She still had her neat, tiny figure, her blonde hair with its Edwardian coiffure of little curls and ringlets, her flawless skin and clear, deep-blue eyes. He put his arm round her, almost scooping her up like a small child, she was so fragile.

"I have an idea," she went on, "that the honeymoon was not a great success." She looked up at him searchingly.

"On the contrary," Alexander replied. "It was a great success and I am very much in love, but we did have an altercation which I bitterly regret. Irene thought I was trying to put pressure on her not to go to Berlin and she resented it."

Lally drew away from him, carefully examining the rings on her fingers as if she remained unconvinced.

"I think it was very reasonable of you not to want her to go to Berlin."

"So do I."

"After all she is Jewish and we know what is happening to the Jews."

"She said she was now married to an Englishman and thought this would protect her."

"Foolish girl." Lally sat down and lit a cigarette.

"I had my call-up papers today." Alexander perched on the arm of her chair.

"The air force?"

"Yes."

"I feel it will be very dangerous."

"Anywhere will be very dangerous."

"Oh *don't*, Alexander." Her arm stole round him. "I can't bear the thought of losing you. I lost my son Roger in the last war and he was the same age as you."

"You won't be losing me. I can promise you that." He bent and kissed her head. "I am very unhappy, Lally. I found someone to love and now I've lost her."

"Oh, I'm sure that she'll be back very soon."

"You would think she would have contacted me. Ten days and not a word."

"When do you have to report?"

"Monday. That just gives me a few days to leave things in order at the office."

"Pieter Heering will take over?"

"For the time being. There is no one else. All the young men will be called up. Mother," he looked tenderly down at her and squeezed her hand, "I want you to go and live in the country for the duration of the war."

"I still hope—" she began.

"I have no hope at all. Things are moving too fast. The country is mobilising."

"But my darling, people are still going on holiday to the continent. My friends the Routledges left yesterday on a motoring tour of Europe. They hope to go to Germany too," she paused thoughtfully, "but, Bavaria not Berlin."

"I want you and Kate to stay at Forest House. Promise me that, Mother."

"But what shall we do about Montagu Square?"

"I shall use it when I'm on leave, and Roberts will be here."

"Roberts may not want to stay here, or any of the servants. They might want to go to the country too."

Roberts was the ancient butler who had been with Lally almost all her married life.

"Oh, Roberts will never leave London."

"I think we should close the house," Lally said sadly, looking round. "After all, we did so before, and you can stay at your club."

"No," Alexander replied. "I want somewhere for Irene to come back to."

"Oh, but she will be back long before that, won't she?" Lally gazed anxiously at Alexander who, however, avoided her eyes.

Irene looked up from her seat at the bar in the Unter den Linden as the young man came towards her. He glanced nervously round before taking a seat next to her and ordering a beer.

"Can I get you one?" he asked looking at Irene's glass, but she shook her head.

"Any news?" she asked, trying to conceal her anxiety.

Ernst Stern frowned. "She has vanished into thin air."

"Then my visit has been futile."

"You must get out of here, Irene," Ernst said in a low, urgent voice. "I hear people are asking questions about you at your hotel."

"But that is impossible," she said in astonishment.

"No, it *is* possible. They will have taken a note of your name and the details of your passport at the border. I don't think you are any safer than Stella was."

"But I *must* try and find Stella. Surely I can help?" Anxiously she lit a cigarette and blew a long thin jet of smoke into the air.

"There is *nothing* you can do. Your visit *is* futile. As a non-Jew I am in a much better position to help Stella than you are."

Irene had the feeling that Ernst was quite angry with her. She was anxious to placate him.

"The man who helped to get my father out," she said eagerly, "I'm sure he can help. He had a lot of influence with the bigwigs in Berlin."

"Then where is he?"

Irene bit her lip.

"I know he has an apartment in Berlin but I don't know where it is. His name is Bart Sadler. He does a lot of business with Germany."

"Then that's not a very good sign."

"It is. He brings goods in and takes Jews out. He has saved a lot of people. He was able to get my father out of the concentration camp."

"Then it's a pity you didn't ask Mr Sadler to find out about Stella instead of putting yourself in danger. Me too, incidentally, if they are after you."

"I assure you I'm not in danger, and nor are you. I could leave tonight if I wished."

Ernst looked round again. "Then please do. If at all possible you should leave this very night."

Despite her pretence of bravura, Irene did indeed feel rather fearful as she left the bar and made her way through the narrow streets of the Unter with their bars, clubs and dance halls to the small hotel which she had chosen at random for its anonymity and discretion. Her family home had been a large apartment in a block in Charlottenberg, but Irene had had her own small flat above a shop in one of the streets off the Unter which teemed with life, especially at night when the lights never went out and the noise of the cabarets and dance halls continued until morning.

Irene was filled with nostalgia as she crossed the streets she knew so well pausing every now and then to look in the window of a familiar shop, at a delicatessen with sausages and hams hanging from the ceilings, its counters stuffed with delicacies of every description, or to sniff appreciatively the enticing smell of freshly baked bread issuing from the door of a bakery. Several shops were boarded up – which surprised her until she saw the Star of David and the word *JUDEN* scrawled all over the walls – a jeweller or a laundry, a tailor's or another delicatessen whose owners were once her familiars. She could recall their names and their faces, their wives and the names of their children and her eyes suddenly filled with tears.

The danger of her situation then really dawned on her. Grief as well as fear made her short of breath and she began to regret her hasty action in coming to help a friend who had already disappeared. Perhaps the real reason was that she had wanted to go back to Berlin, her home, a place she loved and missed.

Irene had crossed the border without difficulty. Her passport had been carefully inspected, taken away and then politely returned to her without comment. That had made her bold and she had made no attempt to conceal her presence in Berlin, telephoning a number of friends and meeting them openly in public places. But they were mostly non-Jewish and the calls to her Jewish friends had inevitably resulted in failure. Many of her non-Jewish friends made excuses or didn't turn up, and the ones she did meet told her she had been very foolish to return to a place so many Jews were anxious to leave.

Things had indeed deteriorated since she had, at her parents' earnest request, left Berlin, ostensibly for good, a couple of years before.

Irene had found it hard to settle in London. The ambience was not the same, and life with her parents in staid Golders Green had lacked the glamour of her bohemian existence in Berlin. But then had come the increasing interest of Alexander and life began to assume a different hue. He was charming, good-looking and rich. In her youth Irene had never been without money and was only too aware that her parents now lived in rather reduced circumstances. Her father, once a wealthy art dealer, had had his stock confiscated and had been forced to leave most of his money in Berlin having failed to get it out in time.

She had known that if she returned to London with Alexander from Venice she would never be allowed to get away. Not only would he stop her, but so would her parents.

However, not for the first time, Irene regretted her impetuosity in leaving as she had and her selfishness in not calling Alexander to let him know where she was, but she had been afraid that he'd be very cross with her or that he might attempt to come and get her. So she had finally sent a slightly risqué postcard to let him know she had arrived and was all right.

Irene reached her hotel and collected her key from the concierge who said, as she gave it to her, "There were two gentlemen asking for you, Frau Martyn."

"Oh?" Irene's blood ran cold.

"They looked like officials." The concierge's face darkened. "Perhaps the police. I hope you're not in trouble Frau Martyn."

"Did they say what they wanted?"

"No they did not, but they said they would return. They asked to see your name in the register and compared details of your passport with a paper one of them had in his hand."

"Sounds sinister," Irene said lightly. "I shall be leaving soon anyway. Maybe tonight. Perhaps you'd have my account ready."

Irene ran up the stairs to the first floor and, unlocking the door of her room, looked carefully round. There was no indication it had been searched. In any event she had only brought a small suitcase intending to spend only a few days, long enough to assure herself that Stella was well and, if possible, urge her to leave with her.

But Stella had moved from her flat and it had taken Irene some time to locate Ernst who had rooms above a bar near the Brandenberg Gate.

Suddenly Irene was overwhelmed by a feeling of acute apprehension and, taking her suitcase from under her bed,

quickly emptied the drawers and wardrobe and packed it.
Then she took her coat and hat and, within less than twenty
minutes of returning, she was on her way out again.

She was about to descend the stairs when she heard
voices in the hall and, peering over the banister, saw two
men in suits and Homburg hats poring over the register
which the concierge had produced for their inspection.

Suddenly she heard her name mentioned and the concierge
nodded and pointed towards the staircase.

Without pausing for a second longer Irene retraced her
steps and ran lightly up the staircase to the next floor.
Somewhere there was bound to be another way out.

She heard the heavy tramp of the two men coming up the
stairs and go along the corridor to knock at the door of the
room she had just vacated. Irene flew back the way she had
come and climbed the next flight of stairs to the top. She ran
again to the end of the corridor, pushed open a door and saw a
narrow staircase which she swiftly descended to the basement
of the hotel which was dark and smelt of beer and something
not so pleasant.

There was a chink of light at the far end and she ran towards
it, discovering to her relief that it was a half-open door. She
pushed it; it yielded easily and she found herself in one of the
narrow streets at the back of the hotel.

Breathing heavily she leaned against the wall and then,
reactivated by a new and very real sense of fear, she walked
quickly along the street towards the Brandenberg Gate and
the only hope of refuge she had.

The concierge eyed Ernst suspiciously as he came up to the
desk and turned the ledger on it towards him, opening it and
inspecting the names.

"Yes?" she asked peremptorily.

"I'm here on behalf of Frau Martyn."

"She's gone." The concierge pointed to the name on the
ledger with an arthritic forefinger. "She left without paying
the bill."

"I know." Ernst produced his wallet and extracted a few notes. "She asked me to pay her bill . . . and collect her passport."

"I see." The concierge held her hand out for the notes, but Ernst clung on to them. "Is she a friend of yours?"

"In a way." Ernst hesitated. "I don't know her well. She's the friend of a friend."

"Well, if she's a friend of yours," the concierge said with an edge to her voice, "you should tell her to be careful. The police are after her."

"Why should they be after her?" Ernst asked feigning surprise.

"Because she's Jewish that's why." The concierge leaned over the desk and almost spat out the words. "Anyone can see she's Jewish, and a British passport is no protection. I expect she stole it. The police seemed to think so. They took it away with them. I told them I thought it was a stolen passport."

"They took it away with them!" Ernst exclaimed furiously.

"As a stolen passport, in order to pretend she was English. She's a German Jew."

"She is a British citizen married to an Englishman. They had no right to take her passport, or you to let them have it."

"Tell that to the authorities," the concierge said sulkily, handing him the bill. "What do you think I could do about it?"

"How did they know she was here in the first place?" Ernst demanded.

"I told them, of course. As a good citizen it is my duty to report suspicious people to the police. You know where she is now?" The concierge's eyes gleamed, perhaps in the hope of earning a few more Deutschmarks for her treachery from the police, and Ernst felt a sense of contempt as well as despair at the greed and narrow-mindedness of his compatriot. Obviously she was in the pay of the police to inform them about any suspect guests.

"If I knew," Ernst said glancing at the bill, "I wouldn't tell *you*!" And after a quick calculation he handed it with the notes to the concierge saying contemptuously, "Keep the change."

Then he made a swift exit in case anyone was observing him from outside.

Irene sat with her head in her hands, her thumbs pressed hard against her throbbing temple. Then she looked up at Ernst who was staring down at her.

"Do you think they *really* took the passport?"

"I'm sure they did, otherwise she might have tried to sell it to me. The old crow."

"I am in a hopeless situation."

"It is bad," he agreed.

"I never thought about the passport when I ran away from the hotel."

"Well, there was nothing you could have done about it. It would already have been too late. You did the right thing to get away."

"Have the hotels a *right* too keep everyone's passport?" Irene demanded.

"It's a way of making sure people don't leave without paying the bill, also of informing the police if they think it necessary. Anyway they can do what they like. This is now virtually a lawless nation full of snoops informing on people to the authorities for gain."

"How am I going to get out of the country?" Irene lit a cigarette, swept back her hair and looked at Ernst wearily. She was pale with fatigue, dark smudges under her eyes.

"At the moment I have no idea. You will have to be smuggled out."

"How? When?"

"I don't advise it right now. The police presence at the border is a very heavy one. They already have your name. Perhaps they suspect you of being a spy."

"Then I must go to the British Embassy."

"I don't advise that either." Ernst sank on his knees beside

31

her. "They are deluged with people wanting to leave, and you have no passport."

"My father-in-law is a member of the British aristocracy."

"I don't think that makes much difference," Ernst said ruefully. "It may even count against you. I think you must lie low for a week or two. They are already rounding up all the Jews. You can stay here for the time being, and when I think the coast is clear I'll tell you."

Ernst, who was a lecturer at the university which was now closed for the vacation, got to his feet and going over to the window, glanced out. He felt nervous, ill at ease, resentful of the situation Irene had got him into. He already had enough trouble by having a Jewish girlfriend and he knew that some people suspected him of being involved in her disappearance, which was not true. Stella, who was a painter, had failed to come home one night and all his attempts to find out what had happened to her had so far failed. The police denied any knowledge of her and hinted that she must have run out on him. Ernst knew that wasn't true but, at the same time, there had been a number of arrests of Jews or Jewish suspects and wholesale deportations from the city.

Irene, watching him carefully, could almost read his mind.

"I know I've put you to a lot of trouble Ernst," she said contritely. "You probably have plans for the vacation."

"I have no plans other than to try and find out what has happened to Stella. But you see that means I have to be careful too. Jewish sympathisers are in almost as much danger as the Jews, so it may be that I cannot be of much help to you either. I am working during the day in the library at the university preparing my thesis. But don't worry. A lot of non-Jews feel as I do. But we must operate by stealth. It is the only way. Later, if I can, I will have a short vacation with my parents in the mountains, but not just yet."

Irene rose and began to pace restlessly around the room.

"It's very good of you, Ernst, but I think I'd better try and telephone my husband. He'll be able to tell me where Bart Sadler has his apartment."

"I doubt if he's still in Germany. All the foreigners are getting out. I tell you what, I'll see if I can find someone who is leaving by car to take you."

"I have put you in an awful position Ernst. I didn't mean it to be like this. I didn't know it was so bad. I was very foolish to disregard my husband's advice and come to Berlin on my own. But I can't stay here with you. It's not fair."

"You dare not go to a hotel either. You can't remain on the street. You must stay here for the time being and then we'll sort something out. But Irene," he pointed a warning finger at her, "you must be very careful. Don't move from this place. It is an area where you are known. The fact is that there is no one you can trust in Berlin any more."

The telephone rang and Alexander leaned across his desk and picked up the receiver.

"Hello?"

"There's a call for you, sir. I think it's from abroad," the girl at the switchboard said, then, "Oh sorry they've rung off."

"It might be my wife," Alexander cried. "Keep the lines clear for God's sake."

"Whoever it is has been trying to get through for some time. I think it was your wife, a lady with a foreign accent."

"Did she say anything?"

"She kept on saying 'hello', 'hello', 'hello' – as though she couldn't hear me. The crackle on the line was very bad."

"Then keep the line clear. Don't let anyone come through and if it is her, make sure we are not disturbed."

"Yes, sir," the girl said obediently.

Alexander sat back in his chair, his face grey with frustration. Europe was hurtling towards war: Hitler had closed the border with Poland; Britain and France had reaffirmed their pledge to go to Poland's assistance; and his wife of only a few weeks was somewhere in Berlin.

It was a late afternoon in August and Alexander, already in uniform as an officer cadet, had come into the office to discuss a few problems with Pieter Heering the chairman of the great Martyn-Heering world business empire of which Alexander's adoptive father, Prosper Martyn, had been a co-founder. The company did business all over the world and its fleet of merchant ships would be valuable to the British war effort.

The door opened and Pieter came in, pausing on the threshold when he saw Alexander's face.

"Any news?"

"She's trying to get through to me. I can't tell you how worried I am, Pieter."

"I can see that, my boy." Pieter sat down and ran his hand wearily over his face. Close to retirement he had hoped to pass on the burden of the chairmanship to Alexander in the next few years. Now the prospect seemed remote. "I can't tell you how sorry I am. Of course our rep in Berlin is no longer there to be of any help."

"I shall have to talk to Bart Sadler." Alexander put his hand out to the telephone and then withdrew it. "No I want to leave the lines clear."

"I don't think Bart Sadler is in the country. No one seems to know where he is. Now, Alexander," Pieter pointed to a thick file he'd brought in with him, "a lot of things need a decision today. I really don't know how I'm going to be able to carry on without you. I am worried about my family in Holland too." He looked gravely across at the younger man. "This is indeed a terrible time for all of us."

The telephone rang again and Alexander snatched the receiver.

"I think I have your wife, Mr Alexander."

"Hello, hello," came the unmistakable but very faint voice of Irene at the other end of the phone.

"Irene," Alexander shouted. "Are you all right? Where are you?"

"I'm all right. I'm in Berlin. But Alexander I am without a passport. It has been taken by the authorities. Alexander . . . I am so afraid . . ." and with that the line went dead.

34

Alexander sat for a few moments gazing at his desk. When he raised his face he looked more haggard then ever.

"She's in Berlin . . . without her British passport, I ask you!"

"What happened to it?"

"She says the authorities took it. What chance has she – a German Jew – without it?"

Sam Turner had been transformed in recent years from an unhappy, rebellious adolescent to a pleasant, willing and capable young man. He had only discovered in the last few years that his natural father was not the vicar of Wenham, but Bart Sadler, a man he had always been taught to regard as notorious, and who had apparently been his mother's lover in the second decade of the century.

It had been a great shock to an already turbulent young man, but the opportunities offered by his real father were enormous and he had embraced them enthusiastically. He had been trained as a builder, so he was of a practical turn of mind, but he had also discovered a talent for mastering facts and, especially, figures.

He moved in to live in his father's large mansion, Upper Park, and the two soon became inseparable. When his father was away on business, which was frequently, Sam took over.

Now he too had his call-up papers and his father was somewhere in Europe which was poised on the brink of war.

Sam and Alexander had never had very much to do with each other. They'd met infrequently over the years at family gatherings. But the two, thrown together by common business interests, liked each other and got on immediately.

"I don't know where Father is now," Sam said with a cheerful smile, "but he'll turn up."

"You're sure of that?" Alexander asked. "You're not worried?

"Oh, I never worry about Father." Sam went to a cupboard and produced a bottle of whisky. "Join me, Alexander?"

"With pleasure." Alexander smiled and began to relax in

Sam's jovial company. They were in Bart's office on the outskirts of Wenham, a once stately home that had been transformed into a luxurious suite of offices. There were very few staff; Bart liked to keep his cards close to his chest and trusted few people.

"Cheers!" Sam said raising his glass.

"Cheers," Alexander replied. "Though I must say I don't feel very cheerful."

"Tell me what your problem is," Sam said perching on the desk. He was very like his father to look at: tall, saturnine with hooded brown eyes and a mass of thick black hair.

"Well, my wife Irene, who is a German Jewess, impulsively and against my advice went to Berlin at the end of our honeymoon to try and persuade a friend to leave. She is now stranded there herself without a passport."

Sam whistled. "How did she lose that?"

"The authorities impounded it. I have no idea how or why. That is all she managed to tell me on the telephone. I don't know where she is and am only hoping she is able to get through to me again."

"And what do you want me, or rather, Father to do?"

"I want him to try and find Irene and get her out of Berlin."

Sam whistled again.

"And you have no idea where she is?"

"No."

"That is a very tall order, Alexander." Sam looked grave. "It's like getting a needle out of a haystack. I doubt if even someone as resourceful as my father would be able to help you."

Three

September 1939

> You can imagine what a bitter blow it is to me that all my
> long struggle to win peace has failed . . . this country is
> now at war with Germany.

After the Prime Minister's announcement no one, gathered round the wireless in the drawing room at Pelham's
Oak, spoke until the silence was broken at last by Eliza.

"I never thought it would happen again in my lifetime," she
said, a catch in her voice. "The last war was supposed to be
the war to end wars."

Carson rose and turned off the wireless. Then he faced
the members of the family who had joined him for the
momentous announcement.

"Hitler has to be stopped," he said. "Chamberlain has no
alternative."

"But what does it mean for us?" Lally spoke almost under
her breath as if asking a question of herself. "So many of the
family are abroad: Connie, Dora and . . . Irene in the worst
position of all."

Agnes Wentworth sighed deeply.

"They will all have to be brought back. Connie cannot stay
in an enemy country a moment longer."

Agnes, who had a complicated history, had nevertheless
been born a Yetman and was an integral part of the family.

37

"But she is married to an Italian," Carson protested. "She is an Italian national. That will protect her.

"Besides, Mussolini has not yet declared war. Officially Italy is a neutral country. For the moment, anyway, she is safe." Sally Woodville was not at all anxious to welcome her husband's former wife to the family home where she was already stepmother to her three children.

"If Connie comes over she is welcome to stay with me," Agnes replied stiffly, "if *you* do not want her, Sally."

"It is not that I don't want her, Aunt Agnes . . ." Sally began, while a deep flush stole up her cheeks.

"It is just that she will cause trouble." There was a hint, a touch of malice in Agnes's voice.

"We are talking hypothetically," Carson said irritably. "Sally would certainly not balk at giving my children's mother shelter from war, would you, my dear?"

"I think I'll go and rustle up some lunch," Sally said diplomatically. "I take it you'll all be staying?"

Without waiting for their reply she left the room and those who remained became silent again. It seemed all too much to bear. All their men were young: Alexander twenty-nine, Jack Sprogett, Agnes's grandson, twenty-five and Sam Turner twenty-six.

Sam's mother Sophie and her husband had also come over for the announcement with Deborah, his half-sister and Bart's divorced wife.

At the age of thirty-six Deborah might have hoped to play some part in the war. Her children were old enough to go to school and she was restless and rather idle since her divorce. She was tall, slim and energetic, blue-eyed, fair-haired but with a discontented expression; a pursed, rather grim set of the mouth which hinted at the unhappiness of much of her past life.

"I think it's all rather exciting," Deborah said jumping to her feet. Then, looking round her at the grave faces, said, "At least it's *something*."

"How *can* you call a war exciting?" her mother asked her. "War is horrible."

"Oh, I don't know. I think Uncle Carson enjoyed the last one."

"I didn't enjoy war," Carson said tapping his foot impatiently. "I saw too many terrible things, but I know what Debbie means. It does have a quality nothing else seems to have. It's the comradeship of war that I enjoyed, not war itself. I hope to be able to do something this time, though I dare say they won't have me in the army."

"Carson, you have too many responsibilities," Eliza protested. "I do hope you won't volunteer."

"I don't think they'd have me if I did, but I'll do something, if it's only as an ARP warden."

"ARP!" Hubert Turner exclaimed in alarm. "You think they'll bomb Dorset?"

From the garden outside came the sound of toy pistols firing and Carson went to the window to see his sons once again engaged in play-acting what, all too soon, many grown-up men were going to enact in reality.

If only children wouldn't play at war maybe they wouldn't engage in it for real when they grew up?

Later that afternoon Carson and Sally saw the various members of the family to their cars and watched as they drove away.

Carson tucked his arm through his wife's and they strolled towards the lawn where the children were playing. Twelve-year-old Netta was taking her pony through its paces in the paddock and for a moment they stopped and watched her.

"She's happy enough," Carson said.

"She won't be going back to Italy will she, Carson?"

"Good God, no! Thank goodness they're all here. I shall keep them whatever Connie says."

"Don't you worry about Connie?"

"Not really." Carson felt a sudden resistance, a stiffening of her body and looked at her in surprise. "What is it Sally? You've gone all tense."

39

"I think you *should* offer Connie a home, if it becomes necessary."

"Here, with us?"

"She *is* the children's mother."

"I thought you didn't like the idea when it came up this morning, and you went out of the room?"

"I went to see to luncheon. I admit I was taken by surprise but when I thought about it later I decided it was very selfish of me. After all I know how fond of Connie you were, and if she is in danger . . ."

"Of course I was fond of her – once. I was married to her. But that's all over. *You're* my wife now." And he pressed her arm tightly; but she noticed he didn't add that she was the one he loved.

Sally Yetman had married Carson Woodville nearly five years before. There had been a fifteen-year difference in their ages; she had been thirty-two and he forty-seven. Yet in many ways Carson had always seemed old. Those who had known him as a headstrong young man, a hellraiser, said he had never recovered from his experiences in the war. He had come back a changed, bitter, sober, but industrious man. He had worked hard to restore the family fortunes mishandled by his father, Sir Guy. He had studied modern methods of farming and increased his acreage so that he was now one of the biggest landowners in the district. He had invested wisely on the stock market. He had never touched a penny of his first wife's fortune, but he did not live like a rich man.

Sally, a distant cousin, had seemed ideal as a helpmate after Connie left him. But, somehow, the promise offered by their early relationship had failed to be realised. In Sally's mind this was because Carson had never stopped loving Connie, and had married her on the rebound.

She knew that her failure to have children had disappointed him, as it had her. There had been visits to the doctor and specialists in Bournemouth and in London, but the longed-for baby failed to materialise. But as Carson already had four children – three by Connie and one, Alexander, by a former mistress – she was sure he didn't feel it as keenly as she did.

People said that if a marriage was in trouble a baby would help to improve it.

In their case they had never had the chance.

Sally had thrown herself into the role of being a good wife to the local squire. She ran the house well and efficiently, she supported all the town's various women's associations and organisations, she did her share of flower arranging in the church, she presented prizes at fêtes and gymkhanas. Yet, more often than not she was alone, Carson was busy with his own affairs, complementary but separate.

And so it continued in their private life and they became more and more isolated from each other.

Today, walking arm in arm round the grounds had been one of the rare moments of togetherness, maybe brought on by the sadness, the worry of the outbreak of hostilities. But somehow, in a way she couldn't completely understand, Sally, for all her activities, felt she had missed out on life.

She was convinced that her husband didn't love her and never had, and somehow this was something you could do nothing about. Love was chemistry and couldn't be concocted artificially.

Bart Sadler stretched his arms high above his head and gave a deep sigh. There had been times in recent weeks when he had wondered if he would see his home again. He had been on the German–Polish border when war broke out and the German hordes swept over it. Taking a hasty detour he had then found himself in Saarbrucken when French advance troops crossed the German border, but they had halted not quite knowing what to do. Each side was waiting for the other to commence hostilities. Later it was to become known as the 'phoney war' because of the hope that diplomatic negotiations would eventually be successful.

Bart's luck had held and he had offloaded his Jews into the safety of Holland and France and taken a boat for home.

Upper Park was a gracious Palladian residence which Bart had coveted when he returned after the Great War from many years of exile in South America, a rich man. It had belonged to Eliza Heering who, finding it too large for her after the death of her husband, had put it on the market. She had not wished to sell it to Bart because of his behaviour towards Sophie Turner, but by means of a deception Bart acquired the property and Eliza had been loath to forgive him.

Everyone, not only the family but people in general, had hoped that Bart had gone for good, and it was with some dismay and a great deal of reluctance that he was accepted back into the community and began to play a significant part in it as benefactor and member of the town council. With Bart money certainly talked; he soon had a finger in every pie, and his wealth steadily increased.

He further alienated the Woodville family when he married Deborah the younger daughter of Sophie, his former mistress, who had regained her respectability by her marriage to the rector of Wenham.

But Bart and Deborah were not to find happiness, despite the birth of two children. Bart found out that his wife was deceiving him and divorced her. He then suspected his son James was a bastard, returned him to his mother and claimed instead his son by Sophie Turner whom he had scarcely ever seen and didn't know at all. This was Sam, who now stood in front of his father his eyes shining with happiness.

"It is *so* good to have you back, Dad. I feared . . ."

"I feared myself several times I can tell you, son," Bart said, looking at Sam with gratitude. For a man with so few friends and whose relationships with women had been disastrous, it was wonderful to find the love of a son he had neglected through no fault of his own.

"You've finished now for good on the continent?"

"Well," Bart screwed up his eyes. "I won't say for good, but certainly for the time being. I still have my contacts in Germany, though our government has forbidden any trade between our nations. Nor does it give a fig about the Jews, poor devils, or what happens to them.

"There are still plenty of Jews desperate to get out. They are being rounded up all the time. But for me, helping the Jews was just a sideline. I am neither for them nor against them. I just don't like to see people persecuted for their beliefs. A lot of people don't like the Jews, but I have always got on with them. They have a keen nose for business and so have I. Some of the best German businessmen were Jews and the country will feel their loss if they persecute them. Lawyers, doctors . . . they are very talented, which is what so many people don't like. What I shall miss is the profit from my exports of whisky and arms. Countries on the continent faced with the prospect of war are now more in need of arms than ever. But, of course, such trade is far too dangerous, and whisky will become scarce." Bart lit a cigarette and ensconced himself in a comfortable armchair. "It just seems we shall have to sit tight until hostilities are over."

"I have received my call-up papers, Dad."

"Have you?" Bart waved a hand dismissively. "I can soon get you out of that."

"But I don't *want* to be got out of it. I want to join up, as soon as possible."

"You must be mad." Bart laughed uneasily and flicked ash into a ashtray by his side. "Have you thought how *I* will manage without you? You are my right hand. Let other people go to war if they wish."

"Dad, I have to play my part. I cannot and do not want to get out of the war. I shall be sent to Blandford Camp for training any day now and then, hopefully, overseas."

Bart rose and walked to the window from which he looked over the acres of peaceful countryside. Even to a practical man with little imagination he could imagine it scarred with the massed tanks and armoured cars he had seen rolling over the border into luckless Poland.

"I don't think you realise what you're in for, Sam."

43

"I can't help it, Dad. Everyone seems to think the war will soon be over and Hitler will cave in."

"I don't think that." Looking grim, Bart turned to face his son. "I have seen what he has done in Germany. He is very determined. In Poland he has driven everything before him. It will soon fall. I hate to think of you being in danger. I had the sense in the last war to miss it and remain safe in South America. I never regretted it, I can assure you. Sam, I'm sure there's some vital war work you can do at home. I can easily pull some strings . . ."

"Dad, if you pulled strings I would never be able to face my friends who are joining up, or live with myself again."

"So be it." Bart's hands fell to his side. "I only fear that one day this great business I have built up will be rudderless. I am not a young man and you are my only hope for the future."

There was a tap on the door and Bart's butler Harold put his head round the door.

"Mr Alexander is here to see you, sir."

"Alexander!" Bart exclaimed jovially. "Tell him to come right in." He glanced across at his son. "Did you know he was coming?"

Sam shook his head. "No, but I think I know what he wants. It is about what I explained to you."

Bart nodded and stood up as Alexander was shown in and came over. They shook hands warmly.

"Bart it is *so* good to see you safely back. Sam was worried about you."

"I was worried about myself." Bart smiled for the first time. "I felt caught up in the crossfire."

"It's as bad as that already?"

Bart nodded. "Very bad. I was too near the Polish border when the German troops swept in and too near the German when the French decided to cross it and make a brief sortie. But then they stopped. No one really wants to be the first to start fighting."

"They say Hitler will sue for peace once he has Poland."

"No." Bart shook his head. "He will want more. He has

44

Austria and Czechoslovakia. He will soon have Poland. Then he will go for the Baltic States, after that he will want the Netherlands, France . . ."

"But France has the biggest army in the world, over a million men."

"If they know how to use them, which I doubt. The French high command is too full of old men. The German army is highly trained, fully mechanised. The Polish cavalry still used horses. They imagined they were fighting a war in another age. There was terrible carnage. Now, Alexander, to what do we owe the pleasure?" He pointed to a chair. "What will you drink – sherry, whisky? I'm having a whisky."

"A coffee would be nice. I am on my way back to London."

"And so you're in the air force?"

Alexander nodded. "I'm training to fly Spitfires. It's a most exciting aircraft, light and manoeuvrable. I hope to get my wings by the spring."

"And my son," Bart turned towards Sam, "he says nothing will keep him out of the army."

"The Dorsets?"

Sam nodded. "Blandford Camp. We hope soon to be sent overseas to help defend France if Hitler attacks."

"And you, Bart?" Alexander looked searchingly at the older man. "Is there any chance you will be going abroad again? Or has the recent experience been enough for you?"

"Oh, for the time being I shall go if and when I can. I don't think I can get any more Jews out. There are few of them left in their homes, poor devils. But while the rest of Europe is still free I must trade where I can. I have contacts all over the continent. All your company's ships are now commandeered for the war effort. It will have to be lorries and they may also be in short supply. Petrol will be scarce. But people still want to drink whisky and wear warm clothes and sometimes there is the odd surplus of armaments."

"Oh surely you can't export armaments?" Alexander looked horrified and Bart put a finger to his lips and smiled.

"Only a few obsolete weapons that no one really wants.

Surplus to requirements, you understand. Don't worry Alexander," he put an avuncular hand on his shoulder, "I am a patriot too. Now why do you want to know if I'm going abroad? Is it Irene?"

"You know about Irene?" Alexander sat down and crossed his legs.

"Sam filled me in about everything and told me briefly that Irene has got herself stuck in Berlin without a passport." Bart shook his head. "That was a *very* foolish thing to do."

"She said the authorities took it. I don't know the details. She only managed to get through to me once. I have no idea where she is."

Bart put his head on one side. "I hate to say it, but maybe a concentration camp?"

Alexander shook his head. "Oh no. She said she was safe . . . well, that was when I last heard from her which was some time ago. Bart is there any possibility – without risk to yourself – is there anyone you know in Berlin . . . ?"

"My dear man," Bart airily waved a hand, "there are a lot of people I know in Berlin and most of them are not friends of Hitler. They would like to go on doing business and getting rich and living comfortably and in peace with their wives and children, perhaps their mistresses too. It is a madness that has happened to Germany."

"Are there any people you could contact, is there any way—" A feeling of helplessness overcame Alexander and, to his dismay, his eyes filled with tears. "Any way at all they can help me to find Irene?"

Bart leaned forward in his chair as Harold returned with coffee on a tray which he poured for Alexander who thanked him.

"I'll see to the whisky," Bart told the butler waving him away. But Sam was already at the drinks table putting ice into two glasses followed by generous measures of whisky. One of them he handed to his father and then joined him on the sofa. It was a cold day and a cheerful fire burned briskly in the grate.

"If you have no idea where she is it looks hopeless." Bart shook his head. "Berlin is a large place. No Jew is safe. Those who are not in concentration camps are all in hiding."

"I told Alexander it was like looking for a needle in a haystack." Sam glanced at his father.

"Exactly."

"I'm hoping that she would know about your apartment and try and find it. It is still there isn't it?"

"Oh yes. It is a nice property near the Tiergarten, but I have no hope of seeing it while hostilities last. And even if she does find it, it is useless to her." Bart suddenly paused and looked thoughtfully at the grate. "But there *may* be a way. I have, of course, a number of passports – Swiss, Dutch. But you've given me an idea. It may not be too difficult to get a Spanish one. Hitler and Franco are friends and my Spanish isn't too bad from spending a lot of time once in South America. I can slip back into Germany, maybe through Italy which is a friendly nation, and Switzerland which remains neutral." He stroked his jaw. "Yes, you have given me an idea Alexander. That way I can protect my business interests and maybe help find your wife, or find out what has happened to her."

"Oh, Father it's much too dangerous." Sam looked at him in alarm, but Bart returned his gaze with equanimity.

"My dear son, if you persist in doing dangerous things how can you expect me to be any different? Maybe it's in the blood."

Chuckling he got up and rubbed his hands together almost gleefully.

"These are dangerous times, eh Alexander? We are all in it together. If I can help you I will. I'd like to. You helped me in the past when your company lent me ships and lorries. I'd like to repay the favour, regard it as a debt of honour."

"But you have repaid it. You got my father-in-law out of Germany. I don't want to be responsible for deliberately sending you into danger."

"No, you have done me a good turn. I can't sit out the war here worrying about my son. Action suits me and I am too old to fight. One or two more continental trips will pep me up. I shall go cautiously, I assure you. France is still free and I have much business in Paris. We businessmen have a common bond, you know, to keep going. Besides, if I put you even further in my debt by restoring your wife to you, after the war you will do me many favours and I shall be even richer. Now, have you time to stay for luncheon? I think there is partridge on the menu today."

Four

Spring 1940

The 'phoney war' came abruptly to an end in April 1940 when German forces invaded Norway and Denmark. After his conquest of Poland, Hitler had sued for peace and continued to try and persuade Britain to withdraw from hostilities as long as he could keep his conquests, but all his attempts had failed.

In February, Private Sam Turner sailed with his battalion to join the British Expeditionary Force in France while his father, having obtained a false Spanish passport, had lingered on the continent eager to pursue his business interests before the war threatened to engulf everyone.

Alexander, having had experience of flying a private plane in peace time, easily gained his wings and was posted to a Spitfire squadron flying out of Middle Wallop in Wiltshire, so he was not too far from home and was able to see his daughter and Lally frequently.

Rather to his surprise, Alexander was enjoying life in uniform. He liked the camaraderie of the mess, the excitement and *élan* of being part of a squadron and, although he had yet to confront the enemy, he made daily sorties across the Channel and along the coast of France.

At Pelham's Oak little changed, though Carson vigorously adapted his farming methods to aid the war effort and fretted at not being able to join up. However, the war was still a far-off thing despite the grim news from Scandinavia, that is until May when Holland and Belgium fell to the German blitzkrieg and suddenly it seemed that war was for real, and not too far away.

Returning to his squadron after a weekend leave at Forest House, Alexander was having a drink in the bar when he noticed a new mess member a few paces away smoking a cigarette and evidently alone. He moved along the bar to join him holding out a hand.

"New here are you? I'm Alexander Martyn."

"How do you do?" The man immediately shook hands. "Douglas Fisher. I'm usually called Dougie. I've just been posted from . . . oh better not say had I? Careless talk and all that."

"I think you're safe here." Alexander glanced at his companion's glass. "Same again?"

"Gin and tonic, please."

Alexander ordered two gins and a fresh packet of cigarettes and then, as a few of his companions sauntered in, introduced Douglas Fisher who, it appeared had enlisted before the war and was already a Flight Lieutenant.

Alexander and Douglas were billeted near to each other. Douglas soon became a member of Alexander's particular group of friends who were all rather younger than Alexander, whereas Dougie was about the same age.

He was an instantly likeable, friendly man of medium height with brown hair, a thick brown moustache and the sort of disposition that immediately fitted in with the men of the squadron, among whom he soon became a popular member. His wife, he said, was at operational WAAF HQ in London.

Dougie and Alexander were frequently posted on flying exercises together, that is flying in pairs or 'finger four' detached sections as they were called, which were now seen as preferable to flying in a fixed V formation.

On his next leave Alexander invited Dougie to join him at Forest House but Dougie said his wife was coming down, so Alexander suggested that she should join them too.

"That's awfully decent of you," Dougie said. "I'm sure she'll be delighted."

On the appointed day they drove to Salisbury station to meet Dougie's wife and stood idly on the platform chatting and smoking, waiting for the train to arrive. It was a balmy spring day and, looking up at the cloudless sky, Dougie said, "You'd never think there was a war on would you? Oh, here's the train," and they stood back as it puffed into the station. Dougie anxiously studied the passengers getting out and, with a cry of, "There she is," ran towards an attractive young woman swinging towards them, her coat over her arm and carrying a small suitcase.

Alexander stared at her hard and as she came up he saw that she was looking equally intently at him.

"Alexander!" she cried. "Fancy, after *all* these years."

Confused, Alexander continued to look at her, frantically searching the recesses of his memory.

"Your face is terribly familiar," he said apologetically, "but I can't put a name to it."

"Minnie. Minnie Beckett. It must be all of six or seven years since we last met."

"Good Lord, Minnie Beckett!" Alexander grasped her hand while a bemused Dougie said at last, "I gather you two know each other?"

"From years ago, darling," Minnie said kissing him full on the lips and hugging him briefly. "How are you, old thing?"

"Missing you," Dougie said gazing at her tenderly.

"You've become even more beautiful." Alexander looked at her admiringly.

"Go on, you tease." Minnie, her hand entwined with Dougie's, blushed. She did indeed look lovely with her thick black hair in a fashionable pageboy bob, high cheekbones and sparkling brown eyes. She used little make-up. She wore a grey skirt and a pale-blue twinset with a single row of pearls round her neck. She looked like everybody's idea of a good sort, an English rose, and Alexander remembered that Lally had once tried very hard to marry them off.

"Seriously Minnie, I think my mother was always trying to pair us off."

"I fancied you then, Alexander," Minnie said with a merry laugh. "But you never seemed to notice because you were in love with someone else. I hear you married her. How is she? Are we to see her this weekend?"

Alexander swallowed and lowered his eyes. "My wife Mary died in childbirth in 1934. I have married again and unfortunately Irene my wife, who is German, is missing, we believe somewhere in Berlin. She is Jewish."

"Oh, I'm *terribly* sorry." Minnie's face fell. "How awful for you Alexander." She put a hand to her mouth. "What a catalogue of disaster, isn't it Dougie?"

"Awful." Dougie nodded his head. "I'd no idea. You never told me."

"And you never told me you were married to Minnie," Alexander said lightly, opening the door of the car and throwing his passenger's luggage into the boot.

They sat round the dinner table on the last night of their short leave smoking and drinking, the last course having been cleared away. It had been a blissful few days, the weather had been perfect and, by common consent everyone had tried hard to avoid referring to the war, though it was impossible to avoid it altogether as aircraft flew overhead all the time and Dougie and Alexander tried to work out which squadrons they were from.

A net was put across the tennis court and they played energetic games. Deborah came over to make up a four and Carson, Sally and the children came one day for lunch, after which Eliza arrived for dinner.

Lally was in her element as hostess. She loved nothing better than to entertain and every meal was like a banquet, despite rationing having been introduced in January. Butter, bacon, sugar and ham could be bought only on the production of ration books in the towns, but there was no shortage of these items in the countryside.

Prosper Martyn, Lally's late husband, had laid down a cellar of fine wines which would surely last for the duration of the war.

Lally had been enchanted to see Minnie again.

"I'm so sad we lost touch," she said looking at the beautiful woman sitting opposite her. "But now that we have found each other again you and Dougie must come often, mustn't they Alexander?"

"Yes." Alexander agreed. It had been a very happy few days and he had felt more relaxed than for some time. He liked his new friends, he loved seeing his family, being with Lally and his daughter with whom he spent many hours alone, trying hard to make up for being the sole parent.

"And you must bring your mother and father. Where are they now?"

"They live in the Bahamas," Minnie said. "I'm very glad they're safe there. Daddy had a heart attack a few years ago and I don't think he could have endured the war. My brother Ronald is on convoys with the navy."

"And no news of Bart?" Alexander looked at Lally who shook her head. It was the first question he had asked on arrival, and now he asked it again.

"Bart seems to have been away for ages. I'm sure he's doing what he can. But I must say, darling, he didn't seem to think he could do very much. However," she leaned back and looked sadly at Alexander, "we must hope and pray. He is such a clever man."

"Is there absolutely *nothing* that anyone can do?" Minnie asked. "After all Irene is a British citizen."

"Which goes for nothing when you are at war with the country concerned. I blame myself for letting her go, well I didn't exactly *let* her go. I strictly forbade her and that is what made her decide to run away. Had I been more helpful and understanding we might have been able to work something out. Perhaps I could have gone with her. Had I known she was so determined I would have. Of course I would."

"But you had to bring Netta back," Lally pointed out. "I

think it was very silly and stubborn of Irene to behave as she did. If we didn't all love her and miss her and want her I'd be inclined to say she . . . well, no I won't say it."

"It isn't her fault, Mother, if that's what you were going to say," Alexander said quietly. "She had no idea that this could or would happen. No one knew that Hitler was going to overrun Poland and that war was so near. At that stage, too, no one really knew what was going on in Germany, or how dangerous it was."

"I think you're very brave," Minnie said, her eyes brimming with tears of sympathy.

"I'm not brave at all," Alexander replied. "I miss her terribly. I'm frightened for her. I've already told you I feel guilty about her, but there is nothing more I can do. I must just do my bit in the war the best I can and hope that when it's all over Irene will be safely restored to me."

A solemn silence fell which was interrupted by Lally who, as usual, looked beautiful and elegant in a dinner dress of soft blue velvet cut close to her figure. The men wore dinner jackets and black ties and Minnie had on a short, summery dress of swirling pink voile over taffeta which enhanced her dark good looks. It was the sort of evening redolent of the thirties, those pre-war years they had all enjoyed when days were filled with sport and outdoor pastimes, picnics, riding and swimming, and nights were for dinner parties, dancing to a gramophone into the small hours and, for those who were lucky, love.

"Anyone for cards?" Lally enquired looking up as the butler entered.

"I think just coffee and and bed, Mother," Alexander said. "We have an early start tomorrow. Minnie has to go up to London on the milk train."

Minnie and Douglas did go up to bed early and Lally and Alexander sauntered out onto the terrace.

"It's amazing that it's warm enough to sit outside," Lally said sitting on a sofa made of basketwork. Taking hold of

Alexander's hand, she pulled him down beside her. "They're so nice aren't they?"

"Minnie and Dougie? Very. They seem very happy too."

"You remember I had my eye on her for you."

"I remember very well." Alexander smiled.

"She told me she had a crush on you then," Lally confided. "But I think she is very happy as she is and you were always so besotted with dear little Mary. Oh dear, I wish you were happy with someone now, darling Alexander. You have been so terribly unfortunate."

"I have Kate. I have you." Alexander's hand encircled her waist but his mind was on the young woman who, in many ways, was becoming a distant memory, however hard he tried to perpetuate it. He had been that day with Kate to lay flowers on her mother's grave, a ritual they often observed together. Alexander never wanted his daughter to forget her mother or who she was.

"Oh, Alexander." Lally suddenly clasped his arm and drew him close to her. "I am so very worried, so very apprehensive about you and the outcome of this war. I can't help thinking we are on the verge of terrible things, these are the darkest days, and you are so vulnerable up there in the sky, so precious to me darling." She leaned her head against his arm and quietly wept.

"There, Mother, there," Alexander said, stroking her gently on the shoulder, but the words of comfort he so wanted to express didn't come easily to him.

For that night instead of his customary optimism he felt a strange sense of foreboding too.

It was great to be back in Berlin, though it had changed, of course. The streets were now blacked out for fear of Allied air attacks and most of the fun was to be had in the beer cellars when, as in days of old, the air was thick with cigar smoke, reverberating with the sound of clinking glasses, music from an accordion or a small band and loud raucous singing as the clientele got progressively more drunk.

In those years Bart's favourite haunts, before he bought his apartment, were the Kaiserhof and Adlon hotels where he had a suite and conducted his business, proceeding afterwards to the beer halls and cabaret; but he daren't go there now. He dare not, in fact, go anywhere where he had once been a familiar face that might perhaps be recognised, and his presence in the capital city of a country at war with his would be reported to the dreaded Gestapo.

It was certainly harder to do business and, since he had returned to the city he had had to be very careful who he contacted. These days people could go either way. Although he enjoyed being back Bart was aware of an edge, a heightened sense of danger, that certainly had not been there before and he was forced to resolve, once his business was done, to return the way he had come via Switzerland and Italy and wait for the end of hostilities.

Besides, trade was poor. He could arrange for small shipments of goods via Switzerland, but the returns were hardly worth the danger in getting his merchandise across the border. It seemed safe enough to make use of his flat, safer than a hotel where passports were carefully inspected and often retained so that they could be checked and perhaps held by the police.

His Spanish passport had been good enough to pass muster at the border, but after a more detailed examination he might not be so lucky.

Herr Anton Lippe who sat facing him across the table in the beer cellar off the Kurfurstendamm, which they used often to frequent in the past, was a person of some mystery, but a clever and astute operator with an unrivalled knowledge of what went on in all echelons of Berlin society. Bart had no idea what his origins were, or where he came from, whether he was for or against the Nazis or even whether or not he was Jewish. In the past he had done a lot of business with him.

It had been difficult to track him down on this visit, but, after a few enquiries, a few discreet messages, here he was, cautious, not smiling, grey eyes warily roaming the room, always on the alert.

Herr Lippe was gloomy about business although there was always a market for good Scotch whisky.

"I'm closing my operation until after the war," Bart said pouring himself a glass from a bottle of the finest Mosel. "Cheers," he said holding his glass towards his guest.

"Cheers," Herr Lippe said lugubriously. "To better times." Then he lowered his glass and leaned confidentially towards Bart. "I think you are wise, Herr Sadler. It is very dangerous to be an Englishman in Berlin today, even with a Spanish passport." He winked at Bart and permitted himself a rare, brief smile displaying an ugly mouthful of metal-capped teeth.

"Herr Lippe, back at my apartment I have a case of the best Scotch malt whisky for you," Bart said. "It is a sign of my appreciation for the work we have done together in the past, but as I know you have many contacts among the authorities I have one final favour to ask you."

"Do ask." Herr Lippe's face by now was grey and expressionless.

"You remember you were able to obtain the release of Herr Schwartz from Sachenhausen Concentration Camp?"

Herr Lippe half closed his eyes and then nodded.

"Ah yes."

"Well, I am sorry to say that his daughter, who is married to a friend of mine, has got herself in a similar situation."

"She is in Sachenhausen Concentration Camp?" Herr Lippe raised his eyebrows and lit another of the endless chain of cigarettes he seemed to consume every day.

"No. She is in Berlin."

"She is Jewish and didn't get out of Berlin?" A look of astonishment momentarily enlivened Herr Lippe's inscrutable features.

"She came *back* to Berlin."

Herr Lippe whistled.

"Exactly. The foolish woman tried to help a friend and then got caught herself. Somehow she lost her passport."

"And you want me to help you get her out?" Herr Lippe whistled under his breath again as though to emphasise the magnitude of the task.

"I want you to find her for me. She is somewhere here in Berlin, but we don't know where. If you can manage to find her I may be able to smuggle her out with me."

"Give me your address," Herr Lippe said producing a grubby notebook, "and I'll see what I can do."

Irene felt herself trembling as she pressed the doorbell of the apartment in a block on the far side of the Tiergarten, unsure as to whether or not she was falling into a trap. A message had come for her, purporting to be from Bart Sadler, but she knew it was not from him but from someone supposedly acting on his behalf.

It was a chance she had to take. Perhaps her last chance. She pressed the bell again and then stood back as the door slowly opened revealing the strangely sinister silhouette of a man.

"Irene," he whispered.

"Bart!" she hissed back.

"Yes it's me. It's me." He grasped her by the shoulder and drew her inside. Then he locked and bolted the door before putting on the light in the hall and gazing at her. "Irene, are you all right?"

"Frightened," she said leaning against him, almost sobbing with relief.

He put an arm round her shoulder and then led her into a sparsely furnished living room with drawn curtains, lit by a single light.

"I'm frightened myself," he murmured going over to a table on which there were several bottles. "Berlin is a scary place. Very, very scary." He turned to her. "Whisky, Irene?"

"I don't . . ." she hesitated. "Well, yes, I will. Thank you Bart."

As he handed her the glass she looked intently at him. "It is so *good* to see you. You don't know how good."

"Sit down, sit down," he said. Then taking a chair opposite

her he looked at her earnestly "Irene, I don't know how much I can help you. You have no passport?"

"My hotel kept it. Then they said the police had taken it."

"I am here on a Spanish passport. Frankly I am very nervous too." Bart took a sip of his whisky as though to lend emphasis to his remark. "It isn't like me at all to feel like this. But, frankly, I don't want to stay too long. I am forced to be suspicious of everyone, even those people I did business with and trusted before the war."

"But how did you find me?"

Relaxing a little, Irene slowly unfastened her coat. The strong liquor had brought a flush to her cheeks. Bart thought she had changed a great deal since he had last seen her; no longer vibrant and beautiful but a pale thin ghost, a very frightened woman.

"I have a business acquaintance called Anton Lippe. He got your father out of the concentration camp. He has always had close links with the authorities, I don't know how or why. He is a fixer, a clever, maybe unscrupulous, mysterious man. I said I had a case of whisky for him if he could trace you. He told me he thought he knew somebody who knew somebody else who might help . . . obviously it led to you."

"I hope it doesn't put Ernst in danger – the man who is sheltering me," she explained. "He was the boyfriend of the girl I came to help. She had already been arrested or something. Anyway she disappeared. I have been in his flat now for six months and I'm nearly going crazy."

"I must get you a passport." Bart jotted something down on a piece of paper. "Any passport will do. It means that I have to see Herr Lippe again, but it shouldn't take more than a day or two. I hope then we can leave together."

"You mean you can *really* get me out of here?" Irene's tired eyes suddenly shone with hope.

Bart held up a warning hand.

"I don't promise. I don't promise anything. It is a very tricky, very dangerous situation; but I promised Alexander."

"Oh, how *is* Alexander?" Irene's voice shook with emotion.

"He is a pilot in the RAF. I saw him briefly only a few weeks ago and told him I was ready for the mission which I have been planning for some months, but the fall of Holland and Belgium nearly scuppered my plans. It took me longer than I thought. But he thinks about you daily and sent you all his love and this . . ." Bart reached inside his breast pocket and drew out a white envelope. "It is a letter for you; but read it later, and then make sure you destroy it. We must discuss—"

His sentence was abruptly interrupted by a prolonged ring on the doorbell, followed by a loud banging on the door.

"Were you followed?" Bart said urgently.

"No, I'm sure I wasn't. I came a long way round. I—"

"Go into my bedroom, get under the bed, into the wardrobe, anywhere out of sight. If it's the police I'll bluster. Quick Irene, it's the only chance we have."

He opened the door of his bedroom, pushed her in and shut it again. Then he quickly took the two whisky glasses into the kitchen, washed them, wiped them and put them away when the banging started again, this time louder and more insistent.

He straightened his tie, smoothed back his hair and went into the small hall, drew back the bolt and unlocked the door. Two uniformed members of the Gestapo stood outside.

"Herr Sadler—" one began.

"You are mistaken," Bart said in good German. "I am Xavier Suarez from Barcelona."

"I think you are Mr Bartholomew Sadler from England," the first officer said, pushing past him. Then he stood in the centre of the sitting room and looked around. "You are alone?"

"Quite alone. I was just going to bed."

The second officer opened the bedroom door, glanced around and pulled it to again. Then he cursorily inspected the bathroom and the kitchen.

"Get your coat on Mr Sadler, Jew lover, we want to ask you a few questions at Gestapo Headquarters."

"But I assure you I am not the person you think. I . . ."

The officer gestured towards the door and Bart followed his gaze. There, with an apologetic half smile on his face and a slight deprecatory movement of the shoulders, out of the shadows stepped Anton Lippe.

Irene waited until she heard the front door close and then cautiously opened the door of the wardrobe and, still unable to believe that her presence hadn't been detected, went swiftly to the window. Drawing aside the curtain she saw Bart and his escort climb into a car and, after a few moments, drive away.

On the pavement, also watching the car, stood another man just putting a cigarette to his lips. After a while, he turned sharply in the opposite direction and was soon out of sight.

Irene ran across the floor of the apartment and gingerly opened the front door fully expecting to find a policeman outside waiting for her. She had heard everything that had been said, and was sure a trap had been set to catch Bart. Maybe she had been followed. But if so, surely they would have searched the apartment and found her in a very short time? It seemed that it was him they were after, not her.

Jew lover they'd called him. Bart had been betrayed by someone, that was for sure.

She shut the door, looked both ways along the dimly lit corridor and, still shaking with fear, made her way downstairs to the entrance.

Scarcely daring to breathe she peered outside. There was not a soul on the wet empty streets. It was nearly 2 a.m. A woman alone at night would be an object of suspicion and she hurried towards the Tiergarten and the shelter of the trees.

She had not the slightest idea what she should do now or where she should go fearing that Ernst, like Bart, might also be in Gestapo hands.

Five

Summer 1940

F ollowing the invasion of Belgium and Holland the tide of war continued to turn relentlessly against the Allied armies as the German panzerkorps swept all before them and the German 7th Armoured Division, commanded by General Rommel, penetrated deep into France. British armed forces attacked the German salient at Arras but were forced back to their original positions until finally they had to evacuate the town.

By the end of May the Belgian and French armies, as well as most of the British Expeditionary Forces, were surrounded and fell back on Dunkirk while being relentlessly attacked from the air by German Stukas.

Ships from the British navy came to the rescue of the beleagured armies, but the call went out for anyone with a boat to make for Dunkirk and help save the third of a million desperate men gathered on the beaches.

Jack Sprogett's unhappy and poverty-stricken early childhood had been abruptly transformed when his mother Elizabeth discovered she was the illegitimate daughter of Sir Guy Woodville and Agnes Wentworth.

The family had been plucked from poverty by Carson who, up until then, had no idea of his half-sister's existence. Carson was by nature the kindest of men, some said too kind, and his home and purse were always open to those in need of shelter and succour.

Having flourished in a style to which she quickly became accustomed, Elizabeth – who was as selfish and imperious as her mother – subsequently married a solicitor, Graham Temple, and lived in comfortable circumstances in a large house near Blandford. For most of the time she chose to ignore her Woodville relations and her natural mother, Agnes, who she held responsible for all her woes.

Jack was an engaging, if rather withdrawn, young man of twenty-six who still lived with his mother and stepfather for whom he worked as an articled clerk.

To his chagrin Jack had been turned down for military service because of a suspected heart murmur, which pleased his mother but left him feeling useless and humiliated as all his young friends streamed off to the war.

Accordingly, when in May the War Minister Anthony Eden appealed for all men between the ages of seventeen and sixty-five to join a volunteer defence force, Jack didn't hesitate and presented himself at headquarters in Blandford. There he found his uncle, Carson, a retired major, in charge of proceedings and energetically preparing the local force to do its duty, if need be with their lives, to repel the enemy.

One morning towards the end of May Jack was summoned from his breakfast to take a phone call from Carson whose voice fairly hummed with excitement.

"Jack?"

"Yes, Uncle Carson?"

"Your boat in Poole Harbour. Is it serviceable?"

"For what?"

"To go over to Dunkirk and help rescue our boys stranded on the beaches. I've had an urgent request from London."

"Well," sensing the magnitude of the task Jack hesitated, "it's not very big."

"It doesn't matter how big it is. Does it work? I'll come and pick you up in an hour."

"I'll have to talk to Father," Jack said weakly, but Carson

had already rung off. Jack made his way slowly back to the breakfast room where Graham sat with his head in the newspaper while Elizabeth poured the tea.

"Who was that, dear?" she asked turning her head.

"Uncle Carson, Mother."

"Oh? What did he want?"

"Well," Jack sank into his chair and looked nervously at his stepfather, "he wants to use my boat to rescue the soldiers stranded in Dunkirk."

"What?" Graham put his head over the top of the paper.

"He says a call has gone out for everyone with a boat to help rescue the men."

"But yours is a tiny yacht, dear," Elizabeth said dubiously. "Besides can Carson sail it? I didn't know he could."

Jack felt his courage returning, "I'll have to go with him, of course."

"But you can't possibly." Elizabeth banged the cosy on the teapot. "Not with your heart condition."

"You know my heart has never given me any trouble, Mother. It's just what the doctors say."

"Well if you're not fit for active service you're certainly not fit to sail a small boat across the Channel which is being bombed to bits by the Germans. I won't hear of you putting yourself in such danger. I'm surprised at Carson even asking such a thing."

"Uncle Carson said he would be here in an hour, Mother." Jack squirmed. "What shall I tell him?"

"I'll tell him 'no'," Elizabeth said firmly, "if you're such a coward. I never heard of anything so ridiculous. You'd be shot out of the water and killed."

Graham, who had been listening to the conversation, put his paper on one side and his arms on the table. "I think Jack should do as Carson asks, Elizabeth. I'm proud of the boy. He's no coward, just the opposite." Graham rose and put his hand on Jack's shoulder. "Well done, Jack. When duty calls you don't hesitate."

Jack lowered his head and blushed.

"Thank you, Father. I'd like to have a go."

"Carson will look after him," Graham said briskly trying to reassure his wife. "Carson is a very capable man."

"Carson will be in no position to look after him," Elizabeth said heatedly. "He can't even sail, can he Jack?"

"But I can sail, Mother."

"But do you realise what danger you'll be in?"

Jack's pale face again coloured with anticipation.

"I'll be doing my bit for the war, Mother. Please don't try and stop me."

"You should be proud of him dear," Graham said stooping to kiss Elizabeth's cheek. "I am."

"I shan't have a moment's peace," Elizabeth said tearfully, "until he gets back safely. And if anything happens to my boy, Carson Woodville will pay dearly for it."

If ever there was an inferno this was it, Carson thought not for the first time as Jack, the sails of his craft already in tatters, moved her close up to the beach which was crowded with men running towards the boats as they came inshore. The deafening noise of screaming planes engaged in deathly combat overhead vied with the massive roar of gunfire coming from the shore. There British artillery tried to hold off the German enemy whose task had been made easier by the collapse of Belgium, leaving a vast gap between the French and British armies which they poured through.

A huge pall of smoke in the sky almost obscured the sun. The hulls of many boats stuck out of the sea which was thick with floating corpses. Three British destroyers had been sunk and six more badly damaged and the Admiralty had issued orders that all modern destroyers should withdraw from the area.

This was the fourth run Jack and Carson had made in two days, the tiny little craft plying manfully across the Channel with its cargo of defeated, and sometimes seriously wounded, men. Two had died on the way home.

They had scarcely slept or paused to unload their human

cargo on the other side before returning to Dunkirk, Carson at the helm Jack operating the sails. This must surely be their last trip, the jib was torn and the mainsail fluttered helplessly in the wind, so the boat had to be driven by a small outboard motor and was already taking in water.

The two men spoke little as they went about their task, but a strong camaraderie had grown up between them and Carson's respect for Jack, whom he had always slightly despised, now knew no bounds. It had become gratifyingly clear to him that Jack, contrary to the impression he made, was a tough-minded, determined character and not the weakling he had taken him for. He resolved to advise him to break away from his mother's apron strings and start a new life as soon as he could. Jack had shown a strength of character and qualities of almost superhuman endurance which had amazed and gratified his uncle.

Suddenly, through the smoke a group of men carrying another struggled towards them, their faces blackened with fatigue and the dirt and grime of war. One was near collapse and, reaching out, Carson hauled him into the boat. Then dropping anchor, he and Jack jumped into the sea and began to help the others aboard.

"Quick, quick," Jack urged them looking at the threatening skies thick with smoke and tracer bullets as RAF planes recklessly engaged the enemy. Every now and then a plane, flames pouring from it, took a nosedive into the sea. It was almost a miracle that they hadn't been hit, though the hull was pitted with bullet holes through which the water was able to seep, which made a perpetual baling-out operation necessary.

It had seemed as though someone was smiling on them during the last few days as they sailed perilously close to the shore dodging the repeated bombardment from batteries along the coast as far as Calais. This was in addition to the threat from the air and the occasional German U-boat surfacing and spraying death upon the water. Jack pushed the last man aboard and was preparing to jump in after him when he stubbed his foot against something squelchy and, looking down, saw the body of a British soldier lodged between him and the boat. He bent to move it out of the way and then saw signs of movement: the man tried to raise an arm. Jack called urgently to Carson, "This one's alive!"

"We've no more room," Carson shouted. "We'll capsize. You'll have to leave him."

"I can't," Jack shouted back. "I can't do that," and, calling to the last fit soldier aboard to help him he raised the man from the water and, between them, they lowered him over the side of the boat resting him gently on deck.

Then Carson kicked the outboard motor into life and they sped out to sea. The boat was overloaded keeling heavily to starboard, slowing their progress. Two men had constantly to bale out to prevent the boat sinking lower in the water, and the heavy swell of the Channel, the waves crested with foam, seemed a frightening and formidable obstacle. To increase their misery several of the soldiers were sick, adding to the stench of oil and smoke that drifted over from the coast.

There were a few provisions on board, flasks of tea, cake and cigarettes which Jack distributed as the soldiers who were still fit saw to their wounded comrades.

The man Jack had rescued last lay inert on the deck with his eyelids closed. He was covered with a thick layer of oil and mud that completely obscured his features. One of his legs was bent at an awkward angle under him and his other arm seemed completely useless. Jack knelt beside him, carefully putting his hand to support the man's head and held a mug of hot tea to his lips.

The man opened his eyes but had difficulty focusing. However, he eagerly opened his mouth and gulped the welcome liquid, perhaps his first nourishment for days. Then he flopped back on the deck as though the effort had been too much for him.

"Do you think he'll be all right?" Carson asked bending over the man while one of the soldiers took the tiller.

"He's in a very bad way." Jack put a finger on the pulse

at the man's neck. "But he's young and I think he'll make it."

Carson screwed up his eyes and studied his face, gently wiping some of the grime away with a rag. Then he leaned even closer to inspect the victim and there was a catch in his voice as he looked up at Jack.

"It's Sam, Sam Turner!" Putting his mouth close to Sam's ear he said, "Sam, it's Carson. Carson and Jack. You're safe. You're on your way back to Blighty. You'll be all right, boy."

Sam's eyes fluttered again, but did not open. He raised his good arm, groped for Carson's hand and gently squeezed it. Carson and Jack exchanged joyous glances.

This was the best, the most reassuring thing that could have happened as far as the two men, his uncle and his cousin, kneeling beside him were concerned: Sam would live.

Crouching beside the wireless at their home near Rheims on 17 June, Dora and Jean Parterre listened to the new leader of France, the revered Marshal Petain, hero of the 1914–18 War, telling his fellow countrymen that he was negotiating with Germany for an armistice.

Before he had finished Jean switched off the wireless with an oath.

"Armistice! Knee-grovelling surrender. We are completely and utterly humiliated. We are finished."

The Germans were already in Paris, the army set to defend it having scattered. Its citizens were fleeing in droves and the French government had moved its headquarters to Bordeaux.

The situation was made all the more unreal by the normality of the scene outside, here in Champagne. It was a beautiful day and the tiny little grapes were forming on Jean's beloved vines. Would they ever ripen and be made into fine wine? In the yard the hens clucked contentedly watched by the family cats basking in the sun. To pit this tranquillity besides the undoubted horrors of war, the scenes of carnage and devastation in northern France and Dunkirk required an almost superhuman feat of imagination.

Dora felt exhausted. The last weeks had been dreadful as the news got worse and worse, with the German army sweeping all before it. The miracle was that so many British and Allied soldiers had escaped from France and would live, if necessary, to fight again. Mussolini had entered the war on the side of Germany so now there were fears too for Connie and Paolo.

"Thank goodness Carson's children are in the country with him." Dora lit a cigarette with a shaking hand.

Jean put a hand on her shoulder.

"You must join him too. You and Louise. You must leave today. The Germans will soon be in occupation of the whole country."

"I will not leave you, Jean." Dora reached out for his hand. "I will never leave you."

"You must go, for Louise's sake. I will never forget what the Bosch did to women and children in the last war. I will drive you myself to Marseilles or Toulon. And we must find a ship there. To go north is hopeless, it is completely overrun by the Germans."

"Jean, I won't go."

"I order you to go," he said fixing her with a stern gaze. "If not for yourself think of our daughter and what will happen to her."

Following the fall of France the Prime Minister Winston Churchill, who was instilling a new feeling of resolution in a people still reeling from the catastrophe of Dunkirk, told the nation that the battle of France had ended and the battle of Britain had begun.

He spoke prophetically. On 11 August the Luftwaffe began a prolonged and sustained offensive against Britain beginning with the south-east coastal towns and shipping on the English Channel, and then proceeding inland.

The Germans thought that four days would be enough to

destroy British air defences, and four weeks would finish off the RAF. They reckoned without the Spitfires and Hurricane aeroplanes, the men who flew them, and radar which could detect enemy planes long before they appeared.

In the thick of the fight to save England was the squadron to which Alexander Martyn was attached, and by mid August he already counted three enemy fighters shot down and a bomber damaged among his kill. With the advantage of radar the RAF planes were no longer obliged to take to the air at the first indication of the approach of enemy aircraft but could zoom up to the attack when they were in sight. The aim was to engage the fighters escorting the enemy bombers with Spitfires, scatter them and then home in on the defenceless bombers with Hurricanes.

Soon Alexander began to feel almost as at home in the air as he was on the ground. He had found his *métier*, disregarded the danger and enjoyed every moment. To this was added an uncharacteristic recklessness which somehow seemed to arise from his despair at the strange disappearance of Bart Sadler, and the feeling, as a consequence, that he had lost Irene for good. It was nearly a year since her disappearance and their first wedding anniversary came and went without any celebration.

Between raids the men enjoyed a camaraderie that was unique, as if a feeling of shared danger enhanced life and made them live every moment to the full.

Alexander and Dougie were almost inseparable and, when possible, either went up to London to join Minnie or they all went to Forest House to be spoilt by Lally. It was a curious but workable threesome because, as a married man, even if he hadn't seen his wife for a year, Alexander didn't want to become entangled emotionally, and war was a very emotional time. He was able to have fun and enjoy himself with Dougie, Minnie and their friends without complications.

In a very short time they all became attuned to a way of life it would have been impossible to imagine only a few months earlier.

Alexander was reading in his room when the buzzer to action stations sounded. He leapt up and made for the briefing room where most of his squadron had already gathered, some tugging on their flying suits or having a final puff at their cigarettes.

Dougie was already there standing by the squadron leader and Alexander joined him.

"I hope we won't be long," Alexander said.

"Oh, plenty of time for that!" Dougie consulted his watch. They were due to go up to London for a birthday party picking up Minnie on the way.

"Good luck old boy," Dougie said as, the briefing over, they made for their craft. Then, as if he had had a sudden thought, he said, "Oh, and look, if anything should ever happen . . ."

"Nothing will," Alexander said firmly, fastening his helmet.

But still Dougie hesitated. "If it should, you know . . . see that Minnie's all right will you?"

"See you tonight," Alexander called above the noise made by the propellers as they sprang into life.

It was a cloudless sky and Alexander looked down at the countryside of Dorset and Wiltshire far beneath him. Dotted with sheep and cattle grazing contentedly it was an idyllic, peaceful scene. Yet it was midsummer in an England traumatised by war.

As he climbed higher he could see the Channel and then a wave of enemy bombers appearing like a sinister swarm of giant bees homing in with the object of attacking his beloved land.

The sight of the enemy bent on destruction always filled Alexander's heart with hatred and he squared his jaw, his thumb on the gun button ready to fire as the German fighters flew above the bombers to confront the Spitfires.

As dogfights developed the battle became furious. The enemy Dornier bombers droned on out of sight while their protectors tried to shake off their pursuers. Alexander saw two enemy planes go down and then the fighters banked away and began to scatter. Except for a few puffs of smoke the sky suddenly became clear and the squadron leader gave the thumbs up to his men as he passed them giving orders to return to base. There was some good-natured banter on the RT and Dougie said there would be time for a game of snooker in the mess and a few beers before they left for London. He, too, passed Alexander and gave him the thumbs up.

Alexander, bringing up the rear settled back, relaxed, conscious of a job well done. The sky in front of him was clear, the animals below still safe, grazing as they had been an hour before, the earth undamaged. This part of rural England had been preserved, at least for a while longer. He then happened to glance round and, to his horror, saw several Messerschmitts 110 about 3000 feet above him. They were probably reserves that had been called in and had came sneaking over the Channel. In front of him the squadron continued, some of them well in advance, unaware of the peril.

He shouted, "Look behind you."

At that moment the Messerschmitts broke formation and screamed down, guns blazing.

Alexander, his finger firmly on the button, dived into action as the leading Messerschmitt opened fire on him and shells whizzed over his head. He dived, but was followed, dived again and then saw Dougie's Spitfire edge up recklessly close to the Messerschmitt, until he was almost touching it, and empty his gun into the fuselage. The enemy plane's cockpit covering flew off, a trail of smoke appeared from the fuselage, followed by a sheet of flame and it spiralled, blazing, towards the earth.

"Rather him than me," Alexander muttered. "Thanks a million, Dougie. I owe you . . ."

But at that moment another plane appeared out of the mêlée and made straight for Dougie, its cannon firing. Alexander saw Dougie's plane bank sharply away as he tried to take evasive action. He swooped and turned but the enemy plane followed him as if the pilot was intent on avenging his comrade. There was another burst of cannon fire, the tail of Dougie's plane flew off followed by a violent explosion and the craft, enveloped in a ball of flame, spiralled slowly downwards like a firework until it reached the earth where it showered into fragments.

Alexander swooped low to inspect the burning wreckage but no welcoming sight of a figure ran from it. In moments it was reduced to ashes. His eyes filled with tears. His heart burning with rage, he soared up into the skies again looking for the plane that had killed his friend.

The Messerschmitts were scattering. Only one remained in sight and it was limping. Dougie had at least managed to prang it before it got him.

Over his RT came the command to return to base but Alexander, ignoring it, turned and tore after the damaged Messerschimtt which was trying to limp across the Channel and return to the safety of its base in France. When he had it within his sights he emptied all his ammunition into it. Momentarily he got a close-up of the pilot's face, rigid with fear, and then a sheet of flame engulfed the plane, a wing fell off and it rolled lopsidedly many times before diving into the sea. There was a mighty splash, a furious churning of the waves and suddenly all was still again.

Alexander circled over it determined to kill the pilot if he saw him surface, but all remained calm, and after a few moments he flew after his squadron trying to make up for lost time, sure that he would be reprimanded for disobeying orders.

Alexander, cap in hand, waited in the hall of operation headquarters while around him milled personnel from all branches of the armed services. Yet he noticed no one, all faces were blurred as he looked expectantly at the door leading to the operations room.

It was five o'clock, the time they had arranged to pick Minnie up. Alexander's heart was as heavy as lead. Time for a game of snooker before driving up to London, Dougie had said. There had not even been time to say goodbye.

"Alexander?" Her gentle voice, her smiling, expectant face were a torment to him. As he looked at her, her expression changed and he knew that his own had given everything away.

"It's Dougie isn't it? I knew your squadron was in action and there were losses . . ." Minnie turned away biting her knuckles as if to stifle her tears.

Alexander nodded. "We had to engage the enemy over Portsmouth today . . . Dougie bought it. Oh, Minnie, I'm so terribly sorry."

"Let's get out of here," Minnie said hitching her bag over her shoulder. She looked so smart in her WAAF officer's uniform, her hat half covering her dark pageboy bob.

They drove to her flat in Earl's Court, rented accommodation for the duration of the war. Dougie had said he wanted to farm and after the war they intended to go to Scotland, breed sheep and raise a family.

The flat was rather sparsely furnished and impersonal. Alexander had been there several times before. He followed Minnie as she opened the door and put her hat and bag on the stand in the hall and shook out her hair, her actions all precise, automatic. He put his hat next to hers and followed her into the living room where she was pouring drinks. He held out his cigarette case and she took one and raised her eyes to him as he lit it.

"How did it happen?"

Alexander told her. "He saved my life but I couldn't save his," he said bitterly. "Now I wish I had gone down with him."

"Then I'd have no one," Minnie said gently. "Are you sure . . . he has gone?"

"I went down to inspect the wreckage. There was no sign of life. He must have died at once. I got the blighter who went after him. It nearly got me court martialled."

"Alexander *why* . . . ?" She put a hand on his arm in consternation.

74

"I disobeyed orders to return with the squadron. I've been reprimanded, but the CO says there'll be no further action, and it won't affect my promotion. I think, unofficially, he was rather pleased with me. I've got the highest kill in the squadron. If I hadn't pranged the blighter it might have been a different story. Minnie . . . I'm so sorry. I loved Dougie too you know."

"I know." Minnie's grasp on his arm tightened. "And he loved you in his funny bluff way. He really did. You meant a lot to us both, but oh, Alexander, I shall miss him so much."

And only then did she allow herself to break down and weep.

Six

Spring 1941

Deep in the heart of the Sussex countryside the war seemed very far away, though at night the air throbbed with the ominous sounds of enemy planes droning overhead on their way to bomb London.

The garden was full of spring blooms, and birdsong filled the air. In a wheelchair under the burgeoning oak tree Sam Turner, well wrapped up, looked towards the house as a woman, accompanied by one of the convalescent-home doctors, walked slowly towards him, deep in conversation.

About him, no doubt. Sam put aside the book he'd been pretending to read and looked up as Deborah Sadler, a bright smile on her face stood in front of him.

"You took your time," he said truculently.

"Crosspatch." She stooped to kiss him. "I was talking to Doctor Warner about you."

Dr Warner held out his hand.

"I'll say goodbye for now, Mrs Sadler. We'll be in touch."

"Thank you, Doctor."

As the doctor walked back to the house Deborah took the chair next to Sam and groped for his hand.

"He says you're doing awfully well."

"Liar!" Sam snorted. "They don't think I'll ever be fit to go to the front again. It will be a desk job, if that. A man who can't walk is not much good in the army is he?"

"Sam, you mustn't despair." Deborah leaned towards him. "You've done your bit anyway. Next time you might be killed. It isn't as though you *avoided* the war. You haven't, and you got a medal to prove it."

Sam stared broodingly in front of him saying nothing.

The Military Medal had been awarded for his bravery at the front in saving the life of a fellow soldier at the risk of his own.

The man whose life Sam had saved under a barrage of intense gunfire was now back in the war but Sam had sustained two broken legs, one so shattered it had nearly been amputated, a broken arm, a ruptured spleen, which had to be removed, together with part of a kidney. For months he had hovered between life and death. When he was well enough to be informed that his father was still missing, perhaps somewhere in Germany, he had a relapse.

Now, in the convalescent home, he seemed finally on the way to recovery. The authorities wanted to invalid him out of the army but he wanted to stay.

"Sam," Deborah said, "I want to talk to you seriously."

"About what?" he asked rather belligerently.

"It's about the business. Your business, Bart's business."

"What about it?"

"It is rudderless."

"I can't help that."

"No, I know you can't. But if . . . when Bart comes back, because truly I think he will, there will be no business left. He'll be furious. You are clearly in no fit state to run it. So I thought . . . well, Sam, don't laugh but I thought I might see what I could do."

"You know nothing about business," Sam said with a derisory laugh. Like his father he could be very unpleasant when he chose.

"No, I know I don't, but neither did you before you got into it and—"

"I'm a man, that's different. Men have a much more instinctive head for business than women. Besides I had

77

experience of the building trade. You've no experience of anything."

Deborah looked pained. An attractive, rather faded blonde of thirty-eight, she wore a summer dress of navy Moygashel with a large white bow and a navy straw hat tilted over her forehead.

"Don't be nasty, Sam." Deborah drew a little away from him. "Don't be petty and childish. You're in a very bad mood today, so I think I'll go."

As Deborah rose, Sam pulled her back. "No, don't go. Please don't go. I'm sorry I was beastly. I *am* in a horrible mood today. Despite what Doctor Wilson says I don't think I am making progress. I can do very little for myself and I can't walk. I have no strength in my legs. I'm no good to man or beast or myself. In fact I hate myself at the moment."

And suddenly Sam, strong Sam, whom Deborah had never seen weep in his life burst into tears.

"Oh, Sam!" she said sinking to her knees beside him. "Oh, Sam don't cry."

Then her own eyes filled with tears and she rested her head on his lap.

Deborah had had a lot of sadness in her own life. She'd been a wayward child and, as an adolescent, had run away from home with an itinerant labourer, and given birth to an illegitimate child. She had subsequently married Bart, then deceived him. When he found out he had divorced her.

They had two children, Helen and James, but Bart had believed James was not his son and had disowned him.

In fact James, now five, grew more and more like Bart every day. There was no mistaking whose child he was, but in view of what had happened to Bart, and if he was never to be seen again, it didn't really matter now.

Deborah was a dutiful mother to her two children. Helen was in a boarding school in the west country, but James was at home with her. The son she'd had when she was nineteen she never saw. He'd been adopted by relatives of her stepfather and was apparently very happy. Everyone had decided it was better that way: to make a new beginning. She never ever thought about him now.

Her relations with her mother Sophie had always been difficult and there was little hope that they would be mended. Her half-brother Sam had always been considered a problem and Deborah had had little to do with him. Both Deborah and her sister had resented him and a kind of muted feeling of antagonism had existed between them. However, in time, a grudging feeling of respect had developed between Deborah and Sam, people of similar characteristics and experience, because they had both been rather unpopular members of the household where the favourites were Deborah's elder sister Ruth and Tim Turner her younger half-brother. It had become a case of Sam and Deborah against the rest.

Deborah was a woman who was bored and unfulfilled; a rather spoilt, selfish creature who looked her age. She would have liked to have done some war work, but the jobs available seemed even more boring than her present life and she had little real sense of patriotism. She joined the WVS and did one thing and then another and then gave up.

Sam's terrible injuries at Dunkirk had given Deborah a much needed good cause. He became her war work and she threw herself into his welfare, going to see him at least once a week, discussing his progress, or lack of it, with his doctors, generally rousing him as much as she could and trying to help to dispel his natural gloom and cheer him up.

The thought of taking over from Bart and making a success of his business was a challenge that appealed to her. She had spent far more time in the office than she let on to Sam, mainly in an effort to find a clue to the mystery of what had happened to Bart. It was a year since he'd disappeared and not a word had been heard from him or about him. It seemed unlike Bart to vanish in that way.

"Dad would never have disappeared of his own accord," Sam said as if he could read her mind. "He must have been captured because of what he did for the Jews. He must be dead."

"Don't say that." Deborah had little affection for her ex-husband but she wished him no harm. She dried her eyes and looked up at Sam. "You know Bart. He's probably working undercover."

"No." Sam shook his head. "He would have got in touch with us. He'd find a way. He's dead or he'd have let us know."

"In that case," Deborah slowly rose to her feet and sat down again next to Sam, "I think you ought to let me help with the business until you're fit to take over, or at least try. I think it's the very best thing. Don't you?"

"If you like," Sam said and then, sighing deeply, "Sometimes I wonder if I'll ever be fit myself to do anything again. Sometimes I wish Jack had kicked me away from the boat and left me to drown."

August 1941

"She's lovely isn't she?" Lally, who had been studying Minnie practising her croquet strokes on the lawn, looked sideways at Alexander. Half asleep in a deckchair beside her, he nodded. Exhausted from almost non-stop combat duties he was enjoying a rare spot of leave and Minnie had joined him as Lally's guest. Lally had always liked Minnie, and had she had her way she and Alexander would have been married years ago. But Alexander had been in love with Mary Sprogett and Minnie also had married someone else.

Now only a missing woman seemed to prevent that happy outcome of Lally's dreams.

"I wish we *knew* about Irene," Lally said sitting back and folding her arms behind her head.

Alexander didn't reply.

"I mean whether she was alive or not—" Lally went on, but Alexander interrupted her.

"Please, Mother, drop the subject. There is no possibility

of me and Minnie marrying now or, perhaps, ever. We both know that and we never discuss it."

"I'm sure she loves you."

"It is too early for either of us to think of anything like that. When you have been happily married, as we both undoubtedly were, it is far too soon to be thinking of anything else. Dougie has only been dead for a year, and of course I can't stop thinking about Irene and what might have happened to her; but I won't know until the war is over, and maybe for years after that." Alexander glanced at his watch. "What time are they coming for lunch?"

"My goodness!" Lally also looked at her watch and got up. "They will soon be here. I'll go and make sure that Cook has everything in order."

As Lally crossed the lawn Alexander smiled to himself. Cook would have had everything ready for hours, if not days. A family party was just what Lally enjoyed, redolent of the old days when huge family parties were regular occasions at Forest House. Lally loved to entertain and did it so well.

Minnie, her croquet mallet in her hand strolled over to him and slumped onto Lally's vacated chair. Lying back, shading her eyes against the sun, she remained silent looking about her.

"It is *so* beautiful here," she said. "I can't believe . . . just a year ago, on a day like this Dougie died."

Alexander held out his hand and Minnie took it and pressed it.

"I don't know what I would have done without you, Alexander. With my parents abroad and Ronald at sea I would have been completely alone in the world."

Alexander said nothing but continued to hold her hand. Then, eventually he said, "We both needed each other for comfort. It was meant."

"I'm rather nervous about meeting your family," Minnie said lightly as if anxious to change the subject. They relied a lot on banter to avoid a discussion of real feelings, maybe in case it should reveal too much.

"Nothing to be nervous about. You'll love them and they'll love you."

"I already love Lally, but then I've known her for such a long time." Minnie paused and looked at him, hesitating before saying, "You never told me, Alexander, or perhaps you don't want to, how Lally came to . . . well, I know she's not your real mother."

"I'll take you to my mother's grave one day." Alexander, now thoroughly wide awake, sat up. This, perhaps, was the moment when banter was rightly put aside. "My mother was an ordinary working-class woman called Nelly Allen. I saw her once but then only from a distance. She was very beautiful. She and my father, Carson, had an affair when they were both very young and he was living in London where she worked as a barmaid.

"Carson was ordered by his family to return home, for some alleged misdemeanour, and left without knowing Nelly was pregnant. He tried to find her but couldn't. After I was born Nelly and Massie, her friend, who now looks after Kate, left me on Lally's doorstep just with a note with my name, but Lally adopted me and only years later was it revealed who my parents were. By then Nelly had died here of tuberculosis. Carson had heard that she was ill and brought her to Pelham's Oak. That is why Connie left him. The rest you know."

As Minnie sat staring wide-eyed in front of her Alexander said, half jokingly, "I guess that's left you speechless."

"It *is* quite a tale," she murmured breathlessly.

"I hated my family for a while. I eloped with Mary to spite them. Then Mary died when she had Kate and . . . that just about closes the circle I think. I was incredibly callous towards Lally, and ungracious; but they were all so wonderful and understanding and patient with me that, in the end, it was all right. I feel so lucky to have discovered my birthright, to have a family like this, to know who I am. I have been incredibly blessed . . . but unlucky in love. I mean unlucky in that I loved two women and lost them."

Alexander started at the sound of cars coming up the drive.

"That will be them," he said jumping up and glancing at Minnie reassuringly as she hung back. "Be brave."

It took Minnie some time to work out who was who in this large and rather bewildering family, and they weren't all there by any means. She was surprised at the number of young or fairly young children and then Carson, who had taken to her immediately, explained who belonged to whom and where their missing parents were.

His three children, the older ones, were in riding kit and smiled politely when introduced. Lally still kept a stable as Alexander liked to ride and after lunch there was to be an excursion. They were rather restlessly waiting for lunch to begin, but Lally had drinks served on the terrace beforehand so that everyone could get to know Minnie.

Toby and Leonard were both rather grave boys, almost young men, sixteen and fifteen. Perhaps their attitude had been conditioned by the war and the fact that their mother was still in Italy. Netta, fourteen, was on her way to being a beauty. Tall and grave, like her brothers, she had her father's colouring – blue eyes, ash-blonde hair which was parted in the middle and swept back into a single plait so that it would fit neatly and tidily under her riding hat.

"Jean is still in France," Carson explained pointing out Louise. "He refused to come with Dora and Louise when they left last year."

"He wouldn't leave his vines." Dora, who was sitting near, overheard them.

"Are you able to be in contact?" Minnie asked.

"Only in a roundabout way."

"Perhaps I can help."

"Oh?" Dora looked at her with interest. "How?"

"I can't be too specific," Minnie said, "but I know people who know people."

"I'd be awfully glad if you could help." Dora moved closer to her. "I would also like to get back into France again."

"I'll see what I can do." Minnie smiled mysteriously. "I don't want to hold out false promises."

"I don't want Dora to go back to France," Eliza said in alarm.

"But Mother, I should be with my husband. I want to be with him."

"What will happen to Louise?"

Dora smiled and looked around. "With a family like this do you think she'd be lonely?"

After lunch Minnie's practise with the croquet mallet paid off and she and Alexander beat Carson and Sally. The three older children went riding while the younger ones played under the supervision of Kate's nurse, the beloved Massie. Dora sat chatting to Sam and Deborah, who had now undertaken the management of Bart's business, or what was left of it.

Sam had been listening to the conversation between Minnie and Dora and later, over tea, which was served on the lawn after the croquet match, he made his way over to Minnie limping heavily, even with the aid of his sticks.

"I'm Sam, the prodigal son," he said. "I didn't really get the chance to talk to you over lunch."

"I know who you are." Minnie flashed him her brilliant smile. "Alexander told me you were a hero at Dunkirk."

"No." Sam shook his head vigorously. "The heroes at Dunkirk as far as I was concerned were Carson and Jack Sprogett. They saved my life."

"But you got a medal, I hear."

"They should have got medals too. I tried, but the War Office said there were so many heroes at Dunkirk among the civilians who helped to rescue the soldiers that to single anyone out would be unfair. I was in the army so I got the medal and *that* was unfair."

Sam paused and looked searchingly at Minnie. His pale good looks, his tormented air, both intrigued and aroused her sympathy and she felt drawn to him.

"It's about what you were saying to Dora. I know you

can't talk about the work you do and I'm sure you've done all you can to help find Irene, but you know that my father disappeared too when he was supposed to be looking for her?"

"Yes, I know." Minnie nodded. "And, please understand, I am not engaged in any secret war work. I work for the RAF in the central operations room. We follow and track our bombers and fighters when they are on missions."

"Oh!" Sam looked disappointed. "It's what you said about knowing people . . ."

"I do know people. People of all kinds such as one meets in the course of a busy life. I was not able to help Alexander and I'm quite sure the same, unfortunately, will apply in the case of your father. We haven't any idea, or very little, about what is going on inside Germany. I'm sorry."

Instinctively she put out a hand and pressed his. "I'm so sorry, Sam. I know how much you've been through, but you see there's so little I can do."

"You're very kind."

But he sounded sad and weary like someone who was near the end of his tether.

Eliza said to Dora in the car on the way home, "That's an awfully sweet girl Alexander brought with him."

"You know she's a widow?"

"Oh yes, so sad. I think they're very well suited, though, don't you?"

"Mother, there *is* Irene."

"I know and Alexander knows. We all know. But if the worst should come to the worst, and we shan't know that until after the war, well . . . wait and see, shall we?"

"Yes Mother, wait and see."

Later, after putting Louise to bed and listening to the news, mother and daughter sat on the lawn at Riversmead watching the sun go down.

"I think the war news is a little better, don't you, darling?"

"Except for Russia."

"Well, now Russia has been invaded she will have to come in on our side. Alexander thinks Hitler has made a big mistake attacking his ally, even if it is an unnatural one. Dora . . ." Eliza looked anxiously across at her daughter, "I do hope you weren't serious about joining Jean in France?" When Dora didn't answer she went on, "Were you, darling?"

"Yes I was, if possible. I mean, would you mind looking after Louise? Of course I wouldn't take her."

"Of course I don't mind, but I think it would be extremely foolish, and dangerous, for you even to consider going back. After all, an Englishwoman in occupied France? I'm sure Jean would be furious if he thought you would even contemplate it."

Dora who was naturally a restless person looked wearily at her mother. "Mother, I do want to do something, you know, to help with the war effort. I know I'm no longer young but there is something I could do. I had a word with Minnie and she knows someone to do with secret operations overseas and she's going to contact them on my behalf."

Lieutenant-Colonel Baker had been at school with Dougie which was how Minnie knew him. For the first few moments of their meeting he and Dora discussed Dougie and the tragedy of his death and the sustaining and comforting presence of Alexander in her life.

"He's got a wife," Dora said shortly.

"Oh I know. I mean as a friend."

"That's all they are," Dora said firmly. "Good friends."

"I didn't mean to suggest anything else," the Colonel said stiffly, clearing his throat and drawing a file towards him. Inside was a single sheet of paper which he appeared to study carefully.

"I see you're completely bilingual, Mrs Parterre?"

"Completely. I've lived in France since my marriage."

"Which was . . ." the Colonel glanced again at the file, "twenty years ago?"

"Almost."

"And you have a daughter?"

"Who is over here and will remain with my mother, *if* I go abroad, that is."

The Lieutenant-Colonel closed the file and studied Dora carefully.

"I must tell you, Mrs Parterre, your age is against you. We very seldom employ people over fifty."

"Isn't it better to employ older people than younger ones?" Dora challenged him. "They have more life in front of them."

The Lieutenant-Colonel laughed. "They are also more agile. They can run faster."

"But not think faster, necessarily. I'm sure there is some way I can help you. Some tiny little way I can be of assistance."

"I'll see what I can do." Colonel Baker rose and held out his hand. "Goodbye for the present, Mrs Parterre, and thanks for coming to see me."

Dora left not expecting to hear from him again.

Eliza was overjoyed that Dora appeared to have been turned down for secret work in France. Her daughter had served in the first war and she saw no reason why she should sacrifice herself in the second. But she knew that Dora was unhappy and restless and when, a week later, Dora was called to the phone and asked to go up to London again, this time to see someone else at a different address, she felt a mixture of emotions: satisfaction on Dora's behalf, fear on her own.

This time Dora saw a Frenchwoman called Madame Greuz and they spoke in French, which made Dora wonder if her knowledge of languages was being tested. She had no fears about this as she knew her French was fluent, her accent good.

Madame Greuz was a woman perhaps in her forties. She

wore a white blouse and a black skirt and had her hair tied back in a bun. Her face was completely devoid of make-up but she had fine twinkly brown eyes and her expression was not unsympathetic. She wore a wedding ring but vouchsafed no personal information about herself. She smoked strong French cigarettes all the way through their interview.

Madame Greuz questioned Dora carefully about her knowledge of the Champagne area of France, about internal communications, her reason for coming to England and what she had done since she'd been here.

Dora told her she had been looking after her daughter but missed her husband and now wanted to go back to him, but didn't know how. That was when it had occurred to her that she might be of some help in the war effort.

"But you are an Englishwoman."

"That's what my mother said."

"You'd be immediately arrested and you and your husband's life put in danger."

Dora bit a lip. "You think so?"

"For sure." Madame Greuz lit a fresh cigarette from the butt of the previous one. Then she solemnly looked at Dora. "And you don't know anything about what your husband is doing now?"

Dora smiled. "I know he will be very anxious about the *vendange*. After our daughter he loves the vines best and then me."

Madame Greuz once again considered the file which had grown bulkier since Dora had last seen it on Lieutenant-Colonel Baker's desk. She then leaned over her desk in the stark ministry room where they were sitting and lowered her voice as if, even in those conditions, it was dangerous to speak too loudly.

"Mrs Parterre, I must tell you something and insist that you tell no one, not even your mother."

Dora's heart missed a beat and suddenly she felt overcome with fear. Her mouth dried up and she swallowed hard.

"Something to do with Jean?" she whispered.

Madame Greuz nodded.

"He's been hurt . . . he's . . ." Dora swallowed again, "dead?"

Now Madame Greuz permitted herself a fleeting smile and shook her head.

"No, no, nothing like that, Mrs Parterre. Your husband is one of the leaders of the Resistance in the area you describe, one of our most valued and valuable contacts."

"Then he is safe and well?" Dora's eyes filled with tears. "For over a year I have heard nothing, knew nothing."

"He is safe and well . . . for the present and yes, guarding his vines." She smiled again, almost as if she knew Jean. "In short we are trying to find a way for you to join him, Mrs Parterre, and serve our cause as well." Then she paused and her expression became very grave. "It will be dangerous and you may not come back . . ."

"Tell me what I must do," Dora said leaning eagerly forward.

Seven

June 1942

A gnes had not spoken for days but lay propped up in her bed seeming to stare out of the window, but perhaps seeing nothing. It was hard to tell. It was also hard to believe that Agnes, who had always had so much to say, sometimes in a very cruel way, might never speak again.

She had been alone in the house when she had the stroke, only discovered by her maid late in the evening when she returned from her day off.

It seemed awful to think of Agnes so alert, at one time so energetic, now helpless. One hoped that, as was said of the late King, her life was moving peacefully towards its close. Certainly she didn't appear to be suffering.

Agnes was a considerable figurehead in the Woodville family, a woman with a past who had reluctantly come home to roost in the small provincial town in which she had been born and which she had spent so much of her life despising.

She was the sister of Ryder Yetman, Eliza's first husband, who had been killed in a tragic accident in 1895. Agnes had been an ambitious young woman yet, it had seemed, destined to be permanently discontented, to live a life largely unfulfilled.

She had had a clandestine affair with Guy Woodville, borne a daughter Elizabeth and then abandoned her. She had disappeared for twenty years to return, ostensibly a rich woman and thus had trapped Guy, then a widower, into marriage.

After Guy's death she managed to fall out with Carson, marry a man who was as much a liar as she was, who ran off with her jewellery and left her destitute.

The family had rallied round Agnes, faults and all, as families did. Her half-sister Connie had given her a home and an allowance; various members contributed, kept in touch, came to call. But Agnes had been lonely, even bitter, and now the daughter she had mistreated wouldn't visit her on her deathbed. Her grandchildren seldom called on her either.

'It's just us,' Sophie thought, screwing up her eyes to study her knitting pattern lying on Agnes's counterpane. 'The few loyal ones; the people who always put up with Agnes and forgave her whatever she did: Eliza, Carson and myself.'

Carson came every day, Eliza most days. It was impossible to tell Connie marooned in enemy territory.

Alexander was overseas, stationed in North Africa to support the attempts of the Eighth Army to contain General Rommel and his panzers in the Western Desert.

'No, just a few of us,' Sophie thought beginning to cast off stitches from the balaclava she was making for Mrs Churchill's war effort in aid of Russian soldiers. 'Only a few left, really.'

She sighed deeply as the door behind her opened and Agnes's maid, Grace, came into the room carrying a tea tray.

"Mrs Sadler is here, madam," she announced. "She's just taking off her coat."

"Oh, good," Sophie said noticing the two cups. "It will be nice to have some company. You may leave us to pour for ourselves, Grace."

Grace gave a little bob and turned as Deborah came quietly into the room and sat down beside her mother, her eyes on the figure in the bed.

"Any change?"

Sophie shook her head. "Doctor said it could be hours, days, even weeks."

"Poor Granny." Deborah rose from her chair and, going

over to Agnes, gently stroked her brow before planting a light kiss on it.

Agnes was Deborah's step-grandmother. When they were young Deborah and her sister Ruth had adored their visits to step-grandmama who was full of so many tales about the exotic life she'd lived abroad. She had been in America for many many years; and then there were her jaunts on the Continent, first with their grandfather, and then with the self-styled Sir Owen Wentworth. They'd stayed at grand hotels and gambled in the casinos at Deauville and Monte Carlo.

Agnes had been considered a bad influence on the girls, which seemed to be confirmed when Deborah eloped with a labourer employed on rebuilding the church tower and disappeared for months, before returning pregnant.

"How's Sam?" Sophie asked as Deborah brought her mother a cup of tea and held towards her a plate of dainty cakes. Sophie shook her head, laid down her knitting and sipped her tea.

Sam was in hospital again. A plate that had been put in his leg had apparently made it septic causing him considerable pain.

"Pretty fed up." Deborah sat back munching a cake. "You can't blame him. He's had a really tough time, but they're discharging him quite soon." Deborah looked cheerfully at her mother. "There is one bit of good news."

"Oh?"

"I've got a contract to build some huts for the army. That should keep us going."

Sophie looked with grudging admiration at her daughter. It was hard not to admire someone who, after a largely self-centred and wasted life, had thrown herself into rescuing a once successful but now almost bankrupt business without any experience whatever.

Bart had had his finger in so many pies, it was hard to know which ones. His import-export business had virtually ceased as war engulfed the Continent. The trouble was that Bart had been a one-man band. He had been secretive and had kept few records. It was hard not to suspect that he had been dishonest too, and had made money out of the war by selling arms to the enemy. But Sophie didn't know this. All she knew was that her daughter had had a hard time but appeared, against all expectations, to be making good.

"A contract with the army! That must be worth something."

"Well, at the moment, no; but if we do a good job, and in time . . ." Deborah looked at her mother and smiled. "I'm making progress."

Sophie smiled back, a little wanly. Progress had also been made in their difficult, tortuous relationship. It had been made much easier since Deborah and Bart had divorced, even better now he had disappeared altogether from the scene.

"Oh, by the way," Deborah said as if reading her thoughts, "quite by chance we've found a contact with someone who knew Bart, who worked with him abroad. Bart kept few documents but this letter turned up from a man based in Switzerland.

"Apparently he's still there and Sam says when he's better he's going to try and see him. A man called Anton Lippe."

A strange noise from the bed prevented further revelations and mother and daughter simultaneously looked towards it, hurriedly put down their cups and rushed one to each side of Agnes whose eyes, although still seeming to stare out of the window, appeared now definitely to be sightless.

Sophie put a finger on the pulse at Agnes's neck, left it there for some time and then shook her head.

"I think she's gone," she said with a sigh and slowly she drew first one eyelid and then the other gently over Agnes's eyes, kissed her brow and stood up.

"The end of an era," she said sadly.

The death of Agnes Wentworth was, indeed the end of an era. Love her or hate her, many of the townsfolk turned out to bid her goodbye. After the funeral at St Mark's Parish Church she was buried in the Woodville family vault next to her first husband, Sir Guy. In death she really became Lady Woodville again, which is what she would have wished.

Her grandchildren Jack and Betsy Sprogett attended with their stepfather Graham Temple, but Elizabeth remained unforgiving and stayed away.

As usual on these occasions there was a reception after-wards at Pelham's Oak for all those who had attended the funeral and, as usual, when they left the family remained behind. Carson had had little reason to love Agnes. As his stepmother she had done him few good turns but, being the charitable man he was, he had been gracious to her in her old age.

Eliza too would miss Agnes, despite her ingratitude and duplicity. There were some people who were larger than life and Agnes had been one of them: a trouper, an adven-turess who had probably not intended much of the harm she'd done.

Sophie, a near neighbour, had grown quite fond of Agnes despite her bad influence on her daughters of whom Deborah was the only person observed openly to weep in church. Her sister Ruth had remained dry-eyed. Ruth had married her cousin Abel Yetman and, in the absence of children, had become a pillar of the community almost obsessed with good works which had now turned into frenetic war work. Abel, excused military service on account of poor eyesight, was a valuable and enthusiastic member of Carson's Home Guard.

As usual, Sally Woodville felt out of things. Although she was one of the family by birth as well as by marriage, for some indefinable reason she always felt a stranger when they were all gathered together, a clan which seemed to exclude her. It was not that anyone did anything to her or that any of them were unfriendly. Maybe the reserve was in herself, or perhaps it was that she knew they had all liked Connie, whom she had supplanted, and she was aware that she could not take Connie's place.

On occasions like today Sally would make herself busy overseeing the catering, and chatting to the guests who did not quite fit in, as she felt was the case with herself. The one member of the family who made a difference to Sally was not Eliza, not Sophie, not Ruth or Deborah or Abel's sisters Martha and Felicity, not Elizabeth or Lally, but Dora, who seemed to understand her in a way that no one, certainly not her husband, did.

Dora had been away for months on some secret exercise to do with the war which she was not allowed to talk about. She had returned for Agnes's funeral and it was possible to notice a change in her, an air of suppressed excitement, of nervous energy. Dora loved family and enjoyed these gatherings even when the occasion was a sad one.

The fact was that no one could really feel sad or broken-hearted about Agnes. Agnes had been feared and respected rather than loved; a source of irritation and pain rather than joy, but she was family and the right thing had to be done by her, the obsequies and formalities carried out to the letter. Agnes would have expected a good send-off and she got one. The family did her proud.

Sally had missed Dora and as soon as tea was served she went and sat down next to her.

"It's good to see you," she said warmly. "I missed you."

"I missed you too." Dora patted her knee. "You look splendid, and I hear the WVS would be useless without you."

"I do my bit." Sally tried to look modest.

"And Carson is galvanising the Home Guard?"

"Oh, he's in his element. He's also very much into all the agricultural reforms the Government wants in order to help the war effort. We have doubled food production. We now have three tractors, and much more land has been turned into arable use. The Ministry are very pleased with us and hold us up as an example of a model farm to others. However," Sally sighed, "there *is* a down side. We hardly see each other. Still, I don't think Carson minds."

"Oh, I don't believe that." Dora's voice was brisk.

Sally regarded her carefully. "You look different. Did you have a good time . . . wherever it was?"

"Scotland actually." Dora put down her cup. "It was brilliant. All the people were half my age but I didn't care. It was good to feel young again." She smiled at Sally.

"But, still you can't say?"

"All I can say is that I'm going abroad. Quite soon I hope."

"Abroad?"

"But not when or where. I shouldn't really tell you this."

"Oh, dear." Sally was crestfallen. "I hoped, well I missed you. Will you be gone long?"

"Can't say." Dora looked mysterious. Then her expression changed and became a little anxious. "Keep an eye on Mum for me won't you – and Louise?"

"I wish I were you," Sally said. "If I went no one would miss me. I long to join up but Carson won't let me." Sally began a confiding tone and then paused and bit her lip.

"Go on," Dora encouraged her.

"I often feel that, after the war, Carson and I might divorce, you know."

"Oh, don't say that." Dora gripped her arm.

"We grow further and further apart. He never seems to have time for me so I make do with lots of activity. If only we had children I suppose it would help . . ."

"But you've tried?"

"We've done everything. I don't think it matters much to him but it does to me. I always think Carson married me on the rebound from Connie – that it's Connie he really loves. He once told me – before we were married – that he should never have let her go. Oh, Dora I wish I could come with you to . . . wherever it is."

Dora, still clutching Sally's arm looked at her intently. "Sally you can work on a marriage, you know. I did. I felt rather about Jean as you feel about Carson for a long time. At one stage in my life I was not a particularly good wife. I left him for a time and went off with someone else. But then, after I had Louise, Jean and I attempted to make a go of things and we succeeded. I love him very much and all I want is to get back to him."

"In that case," Sally lowered her voice, "I think I know where you're going." Her eyes suddenly filled with tears. "Take care. Come back, won't you?"

Dora tiptoed into Louise's bedroom and, seeing she was awake, sat on the bed beside her holding her hand.

"You should be asleep, darling."

Louise shook her head.

"I missed you Mummy and now you're going away again. I don't think you love me."

"Oh, I *do*, my darling."

As the young girl sat up Dora clutched her to her bosom, pressed her head against hers. She knew that she could not bear the thought that she might never see her daughter again, a possibility that had been emphasised throughout the gruelling course she'd been on at a secret location in Scotland in preparation for her clandestine activities in France: 'You do realise, Mrs Parterre, what a dangerous mission you are undertaking and that you may never see your daughter again?' they had said.

But somehow there had been no choice, no real choice. It was duty, it was love of her country, love of her husband. She knew that Louise was safe, but that Jean was in danger and he needed her.

However, as she clutched the warm, infinitely precious, body of her daughter to her she wondered if she had done the right thing. Fraught with danger as her mission was, as Jean's was, might they not leave Louise an orphan? Was it fair to her? If it was not, was it now too late to pull out?

Cold and frightened Dora sat huddled in the body of the Lysander as it began its descent into the area where it was due to land beside the Marne, not far from her home in France. She was conscious of the sound of the engines changing, of people moving about ready to begin the swift unloading of the plane. There were two other agents being landed with her and plenty of supplies. The plane had to turn round so quickly to avoid the enemy that the whole thing had been well and truly rehearsed beforehand.

Now she felt terrified. The moment of landing was the most dangerous time: the flight path would be lit up with flares; they would run away from the plane quickly and dive for cover, or scatter; the supplies would be thrown out and rapidly collected by the partisans waiting on the ground. The whole thing would take minutes and then the plane would be off again. Now she wished she was going back with it. The man next to her nudged her, extended a hand. He'd been on the same course as she had. He was a Frenchman returning home.

"*Bonne chance,*" he said.

Dora gripped his hand.

"*Bonne chance, mon ami.*"

There was a jolt as the plane landed. Almost before it came to a halt the doors were opened and, one after the other, they were almost pushed out of the plane and told to run. Dora fell on her face, quickly recovered and made for the shadow of the trees. The moon had suddenly appeared from behind the clouds making the terrain as light as day.

Her heart pounding, she reached the shelter of the thicket and lay down raising her head slightly to catch sight of the tiny figures scattered across the ground as they collected the supplies that were being hurled from the aircraft. Then the doors were shut, the propellers whirled into life and the plane taxied away, rose into the air and began its precipitous ascent to clear the tops of the trees.

Dora listened for shots but there were none.

The scene in front of her was now empty. She was aware of a low murmur of voices and then, suddenly, a torch was shone in her face and she put both hands across her mouth to prevent herself from screaming.

"Dora," a well-known, beloved voice said and Jean crushed her to his chest and hugged her so hard she felt her ribs would break. Then he buried his face in her hair and she put up a hand and felt his cheeks wet with tears.

December 1942

Alexander stood in the hall of command operations headquarters his eyes fixed on the doorway through which Minnie would come or, rather, through which he hoped she would come as he had not told her of his arrival. He wanted to observe her face when she saw him, to know if she felt the same as when they had parted during his last brief leave. Up to then they had seen each other regularly but on a purely platonic basis, as friends, each of whom had endured a tragedy; the loss of a loved one whose memories they didn't want to sully. But gradually they had become aware that their natural affection was turning into something stronger and deeper, and they had left the issue unresolved.

While Alexander had been overseas they had written constantly to each other and, as far as Alexander was concerned, the bond had deepened.

Alexander's feeling of anxiety increased as a sudden flurry of blue uniformed WAAFs appeared at the door adjusting their caps and shoulder bags.

There was no sign of Minnie. He should have warned her. He'd wanted it to be a surprise, but perhaps she was on leave. He was about to enquire at the reception desk when there she stood in the doorway – a solitary figure, immaculately dressed, pulling on her gloves with a detached, preoccupied air. At that moment she saw him too, stiffened, an expression of incredulity, almost fear on her face as if she could hardly believe her eyes. Slowly her expression seemed to adjust, to soften, and she broke into a smile. They began to walk towards each other with a strange almost somnolent gait, like sleepwalkers.

They met in the centre of the hall and stood looking at each other.

"Well, you came," she said, a catch in her voice.

"I said I would."

"Why didn't you warn me?"

"I wasn't sure of the day or the time. Besides," he looked at her strangely, "I wanted to surprise you."

"How long have you got?"

"Two weeks."

"Two *weeks*!"

"Christmas leave. The first for three years. Aren't I lucky? And you? Oh Minnie, I hope you're not . . . doing anything special."

"Nothing I can't cancel," she said lightly. "Shall we go back to the flat and change?"

That night they dined at the Four Hundred. Minnie wore an evening gown of blue velvet cut on the bias so that it swirled around her, emphasising her slim, lithe figure. It plunged at the neck to a deep V showing a gentle mound of white breast and the corsage of white gardenias which Alexander had bought her. At her ears were diamond and sapphire earrings, a family heirloom.

Alexander wore a black tie. After dinner they started to dance and suddenly it seemed as though the war was very far away, or had never happened and that it was all a bad dream.

"Can you get leave?" Alexander murmured holding her close as they danced to a slow foxtrot.

"I can try. I haven't had any for months."

"I thought we'd go to Forest House. Unless you'd prefer somewhere else?"

"Forest House sounds lovely. Lally will want you with her anyway. Oh, Alexander" – that catch in her voice again – "I can't believe you're back, that it's you." He was aware of the pressure of her hand on his shoulder. "Was El Alamain terrible? You were there weren't you?"

"For both the first and second battle. It was vital for the support of the army." Alexander stopped and clicked his fingers. "And we *got* the bastards! It was a famous victory. Believe me it will mark the turning of the tide."

She snuggled up to him again. "I wish you could be grounded. You've been so lucky. Not a scratch."

"I had to bale out over the desert," Alexander said grimly. "They got my wing. Luckily one of our blokes got him or he'd have pranged me as I baled out. I fell behind lines but the following day I was up in the air again. Thirteen kills now, you know. I think I'm to be promoted."

The music stopped and, as couples drifted back to their tables, they remained where they were at the centre of the dance floor, oblivious to everyone. Alexander gazed tenderly down at Minnie, his arm firmly encircling her waist.

"Minnie, I am in love with you, you know. I couldn't get you out of my mind."

For answer she leaned her head against his breast saying nothing, but he knew from the tension in her body that she felt the same.

Lally said, "What will you do about Irene?"

"What do you mean 'what will I do'?" Alexander and Lally were in the drawing room after lunch. Minnie had gone to lie down, exhausted from continuous night-work.

"What if she comes back?"

"I'll face that when it happens."

"You can't marry Minnie you know, much as I'd love it."

"I know, and she knows it too. She's quite well aware of the situation. You don't expect me to give up this happiness just because neither of us can see into the future do you?"

"Of course I don't, darling." Lally went over to him and perched on the arm of his chair. "It's just that I can't bear the hurt. Everyone will be hurt."

"Everyone thinks Irene is either dead or in a concentration camp. They're gassing the Jews, you know."

"Oh no!" Lally horrified put a hand to her face.

"No doubt about it. All the intelligence reports confirm it. They're taking them straight to the concentration camps and killing them. It may be that Irene escaped, I don't know. Please God she has, but we shan't know until the war is over."

101

"I love Irene," Lally said. "I would hate anything to happen to her. The trouble is I love Minnie too."

"That's the way I feel," Alexander said sadly. "That just about sums up the situation for me."

When Alexander got upstairs he paused outside Minnie's door then knocked.

"Come in," she called and he opened the door and found her sitting up in bed reading.

He stood for a few moments looking down at her.

"How's the head?"

"Much better," she said.

"You've been overdoing it." He leaned down and stroked her brow. "Minnie, do you think it's wrong if we—"

She put aside her book and looked at him with that steady, rather solemn gaze that made his heart turn over.

"You're thinking about Irene?"

"I want to do the right thing, by her and by you."

Minnie reached for his hand and pressed it.

"I would never stand in your way if Irene came back."

"I might not know what to do."

"You would. *I* would know what to do." She put her book on the bedside table and held out her hand invitingly.

"Darling, let's live for the moment, shall we? For this time next year we might both be dead."

Eight

September 1943

Dora straightened up to ease her aching back and, shielding her eyes from the sun, looked down at the River Marne which flowed sedately along – a broad ribbon of peace, untouched by strife – below her. On either bank the neat ranks of vines, like rows of soldiers on parade, stretched for mile after mile as far as the eye could see. Soldiers was perhaps an unfortunate simile, but then thoughts of war were omnipresent however much one tried to forget it.

Yet overhead the eternal sky was blue. Birds, unfazed by battles, swooped low on the lookout for pickings of luscious, overripe grapes. Like her, dozens of grape pickers were slowly making their way along the rows, carefully cutting the bunches of grapes from the vines with their sharp *épinettes*, placing them carefully in the *mannequins*, oval-shaped baskets, which would take them to the press.

It was very different from the old days when the vineyards were full of skilled *vendangeurs*, the pickers who came regularly each year from all over France and stayed in huts that had been specially built for them for the duration of the harvest. Many were factory workers who brought their families from the industrial towns of the Saar or Massif Central. There were gypsies with their colourful caravans, students, itinerant workers and layabouts, all of whom descended on the countryside for the *vendange*, the harvest, which was

103

held every year approximately one hundred days after the flowering of the vines.

At the end of the harvest there had been a *cochelet*, a great feast which was attended by all the pickers, their friends and hangers on, when drinking and dancing went on until dawn.

But all that had finished in the dreadful, calamitous year of 1940. Now the *vendange* was a very small affair and though some *vendangeurs* still came from distant parts, it was almost impossible to travel freely across German-occupied France and, on the whole, local and largely female labour was used. The formarly ritualistic and joyous operation of gathering in the grapes had had to be scaled down, the number of pickers had been drastically reduced and everyone had to work twice as hard. The women themselves carried the *mannequins* which formerly had been the function of *colporteurs*, the men who loaded the carts and lorries.

Each one had had their title, their place in the hierarchy and no one had dared overstep the functions of the other.

Now it was different. Everyone mucked in. Not far from Dora, Jean, previously in charge, was himself moving along the vines delicately clipping the bunches which he had so lovingly tended, yet hating the thought that the product of his labours, a fine champagne, might eventually grace German tables and lubricate the throats of the conquerors.

Dora looked fondly at her husband who, at that moment also took a break from his labour, stood upright and, catching her eye, waved. As he walked towards her she thought how much he had aged. His hair was now quite white and his brow furrowed; deep lines ran on either side of his mouth and even his previously tall and upright figure was slightly bent.

The war had scarred Jean irrevocably. Not only the sorrow of seeing his country occupied by an alien force, but the humiliation of the surrender. France had boasted an army of over a million men, yet it had collapsed like a pack of cards due to the inadequacy of the generals and their old-fashioned ideas about conducting a war. He had felt betrayed by the Vichy government and almost from the moment the Germans had streamed into France he had helped to form one of the main pockets of the Resistance movement – known as *réseaux* – in the region, which had already played an important part in undermining the activities of the enemy. Although he had served with distinction in the first war and was a prominent local citizen, Jean had so far escaped suspicion largely on account of his age; he was now fifty-eight. It was not that they hadn't been visited by the Gestapo – they had, several times. And as chief wireless operator working from a cleverly concealed room at the back of the house Dora had several times died a death as the Gestapo had searched the house; but because nothing had been found and they were considered 'elderly', so far they had led charmed lives.

Dora had managed to reintegrate herself quite easily into the life of the household following her covert return to France. Speaking perfect French without an accent she had managed to conceal her English nationality and had told the authorities that she had been visiting her sister in Marseilles when France was overrun.

Finally Jean reached her, and Dora looking up at him smiled. "It's such a beautiful day. Sometimes I find it very hard to believe there's a war on."

"And what a war." Jean's arm encircled her waist. "Thank God we are able to play some small part in it."

"I was thinking about the *vendange* we had in 1939, just before hostilities really started. Do you remember?"

"I do, and it was a fine vintage. The last for some time." Suddenly his manner changed and became brisk and practical. "Dora I have been thinking that we should move the wireless. I have been told that the devices for detection are improving and they are centering their searches on an area very near to us."

"But where can I move it?"

"I think we shall have to move it north of Rheims."

"But Jean, how can I . . ."

"You will not go with it. They are going to send me a new operator. You will be able to teach him or her and then we shall move it out of this area for a time. It will take the heat away from us. That will be a good thing."

"But, Jean . . ."

"There will be plenty for you to do, my dear," he said consolingly. "Never fear."

Dora shuddered. "I *do* fear, Jean. I fear for you. Every time you go out at night I am afraid you will not return. Sometimes I feel that I can't live with the fear any longer. Oh, Jean I *wish* it was all over and peace would return."

Jean attempted to reassure her. "It will, my dear, and we shall be reunited with our precious Louise and your family again. So far we have been lucky. So far."

"Don't talk like that!" Dora felt suddenly afraid. "I feel you're tempting fate."

But Jean was an optimist and he had that most priceless gift: patience. And with that patience came an even temper. He never felt hurried or out of control, even when he was planning the most dangerous assignments, and particularly when he was out on one; then he was a rock, a true leader of men. Jean's outlook gave to Dora, whose vivid imagination often played tricks on her, a sense of strength, and in her more sanguine moments she believed with him that, if their luck held, together they would indeed outlast the war.

Dora was a year older than Jean but she did not look it. Her hair was the colour of salt and pepper and she still had her rather mannish good looks – a firm strong chin, startling blue eyes, an air of resolution and dependability. She seldom wore make-up but her skin was good and unblemished. She led an active, largely outdoor life, and could have passed for forty-five any day.

Most nights after Jean had gone out on one of his missions she sat upstairs at her wireless making contact with headquarters in London and receiving instructions which would be carried out in the following days or weeks.

Doing vital work, like Jean, helped to take her mind off the danger in which they lived and, in a way, life was heightened and intensified for both of them.

*　　*　　*

The doctor completed his examination and put his stetho-scope back in his bag shaking his head gravely.

"The strain of war has been too much for us all," he murmured looking sadly down at his unconscious patient. Then, with an expressive gesture of the arm towards Connie, he took her by the elbow and led her out of the room. They walked in silence along the long corridor of the Palazzo Colomb-Paravacini, down the grand staircase to the drawing room overlooking the canal.

"A drink?" Connie asked, but the doctor shook his head.

"I have other calls to make. There are so many demands on my time." He stood looking at Connie. "I must tell you my dear Constance, that absolutely nothing more can be done for my beloved old friend Paolo. You know we were at university together and I have been his doctor ever since I qualified? I love him and I would move mountains to be able to save him now. But his lungs have given up completely. He smoked too much and this latest bout of pneumonia has finished him." He put his hand on her shoulder and gazed at her sadly. "It is just a matter of time. Keep him comfortable. He will probably never recover consciousness. At least he is spared the horrors we are living through now. What will become of us all I don't know." Shaking his head the doctor made for the door, followed by Connie. They paused on the threshold which led onto the jetty where the doctor's gondola stood waiting. "And you, what will you do, my dear Connie?" he enquired solicitously.

"You mean after he's gone?" She shook her head. "I really don't know. If the British Army gets as far as Venice I may try and rejoin my family in England; but who knows what will happen?"

The doctor leaned conspiratorially towards her, as if he was afraid of being overheard. "While the Germans are in control you would do well to remain indoors. Now that we are the enemy and no longer their allies the Italians are in enough danger, but if they suspected you were English . . ." He pressed her hand. "Better take care."

107

Connie had not loved Paolo when she married him. She had admired and respected him, but it was a case of a port in the storm rather than love. But he loved her; he adored her. He had long admired her, even before her marriage to Carson, but he was seventeen years her senior and it had seemed an impossible ideal.

Because of his devotion, his tenderness, Connie had come to return his love and, sitting by his bedside constantly in their last days alone together in the house, except for a small staff of servants greatly reduced from pre-war days, she was able to reflect on the emotional security and serenity Paolo had brought to her life and how much she would miss him.

Italy had been defeated. On 8 September it had asked for an armistice whereupon German soldiers had occupied Rome. Troops of the British Eighth Army, having landed at Salerno, began their push towards Naples and the belly of Italy. Mussolini had been rescued by Hitler but had returned to establish a Fascist state, an 'Italian Socialist Republic' in the north of Italy.

For the past two years Paolo's health had been delicate. As the doctor said he had smoked too much and he had worried too much. He had once been an admirer of Mussolini, thinking him to be a godsend for the impoverished Italian nation, who seemed to have the approval and co-operation of the King. Now with Mussolini's fall the Royal family was out on a limb – it had backed the wrong horse – and the collapse of Italy had further hastened Paolo's deterioration. Finally, he had succumbed to a serious attack of pneumonia and now lay near death.

Connie rose from her bedside vigil and walked restlessly to the window. Mentally, she was already making plans. There were still German officers in Venice, but the allies were getting near. She realised how much she had missed her children and longed to see them and the fresh green countryside of England once again.

It was almost as though Paolo was already dead, forcing

her, against her will, to make plans for the future.

By the end of 1943 Alexander Martyn was a squadron
leader, an ace with more kills than anyone else in his squadron. He had been decorated twice – awarded the DFC and
bar – but, following another crash in September when he
had been shot down while supporting the British Eighth
Army in Salerno and sustained a broken leg and other injuries, he had been invalided home. After some weeks in
hospital and a short convalescence he had been given a
desk job until he should be fit to resume active service
once more.

A desk job in London was frustrating, but it meant being
nearer to Minnie which was the only compensation as far
as he was concerned. He had been loath to live with her
in the flat she had shared with Dougie and they had moved
back to Montagu Square, where they had been joyfully
welcomed by Roberts who had declined to take shelter in
the country as suggested by Lally, preferring to take care of
the London house.

Most nights when they were not on duty Alexander and
Minnie changed into evening clothes and went out on the
town, dining and dancing at Ciro's, the Four Hundred or
the Café Royal. Occasionally Roberts would cook and serve
them a meal at home. A bottle of pre-war claret or Burgundy
would be produced from the still extensive cellars, and it was
almost possible to believe that this was a world at peace.

They had both worked over Christmas but for New Year
they had been free and Alexander had booked a table at the
Café Royal where they had been joined by a party of friends.
Alexander still used a stick and got round the dance floor with
difficulty, but get round he did, determined to party the night
away. His experience of war had made him intent on living
life to the full, relishing every minute, and he soon realised
that the fatalistic Minnie shared his attitude.

At the sound of Alexander's car Roberts opened the door
and took his cap from him.

"Is Mrs Fisher in, Roberts?" Alexander asked, idly turning over the mail that was on the hall table.

"Mrs Fisher came home early, sir. She's resting I believe."

"Oh?" Alexander looked surprised. "Is she not well?"

"I understand her to be a little under the weather, sir. I offered to bring her tea but she preferred to go straight upstairs. I do hope it won't upset your plans for the evening, Mr Alexander."

"Oh, that doesn't matter a bit!" Alexander tried to conceal his anxiety but, despite his lameness, went upstairs two at a time.

He gently pushed open the bedroom door and stood looking at Minnie in the half light. She appeared to be asleep. He tiptoed across and her eyelids fluttered. He sat down beside her and took her hand.

"Darling? Are you OK?"

Minnie opened her eyes. "I'm all right, really Alexander."

"What happened?"

"I felt a little faint. They sent me home in a taxi."

"You should have called me." Alexander squeezed her hand distractedly. "I hope you're not coming down with the 'flu."

Minnie was silent but the expression on her face worried Alexander all the more.

"Minnie, I'm going to call the doctor," he said getting to his feet, but she reached for his hand and held him back.

"No Alexander, please . . ." She pulled him down beside her, intensifying his unease.

"Alexander," she said falteringly, "I *have* seen a doctor."

Seriously alarmed by now Alexander leaned over her. "Oh, darling, tell me please, whatever is the matter?"

"I'm pregnant Alexander. I . . . do hope you won't be cross."

She looked at him so fearfully that he wanted to burst out laughing. Instead he wrapped her gently in his arms and held her tightly to him. Gradually he could feel her taut body relax and he bent and kissed her.

110

Finally, when at last he released her, she remained with her head resting against his shoulder.

"I was so afraid you'd be annoyed."

"Darling, I'm thrilled," he said, his face alight with joy. "I can't tell you *how* thrilled. I only wish . . ." he drew away from her and regarded her gravely, "well, you know what I wish. I wish we could be married."

He gently put her back against her pillows and strolled over to the mantelpiece. A fire glowed in the grate and he stood for a few moments gazing at the embers.

"With a new life I feel I can begin again." He turned towards her. "We could start all over together if only we knew what had happened to . . . well." He paused. Irene was a name they seldom mentioned. For four years there had been no news. The truth was that Alexander no longer knew how he really felt about her. It was as though she had already died, the period of mourning was over and he wished to start a new life. He and Minnie believed they had behaved as correctly as, in the circumstances and given the exigencies of wartime, it was possible to do. He had really no idea what he would do or how he would behave if some day Irene were to come in through that door.

December 1943

Dora drove carefully along the narrow, uneven road that led to the house, past the rows of desolate, frozen vines now lying dormant until the spring. The harvest had been very poor. Many of the *négociants* in Rheims and Epernay were not even troubling to make champagne. Their vats remained empty of new wine as the Germans made raids on the cellars emptying them of rare vintages. Sometimes it seemed as though the production of champagne had ceased altogether and many growers had allowed the grapes to rot on the vine. Jean had been unable to sell half of his harvest and had been forced to throw it away.

111

Dora had been working all day at their office in Rheims where, in happier times, they had kept a small staff. Now she and Jean saw to the administrative details themselves. It was also a good cover as far as the occupying authorities were concerned.

Jean did not make his own champagne but sold his grapes to *négociants*, though there had been talk of forming a cooperative of wine growers which had had to be abandoned. Maybe that would eventually be revived after the war.

There had been another reason for Dora to work late on this particular evening. Jean was having an important meeting with the senior members of his *réseau*, and the trainee wireless operator, 'Mathilde' – a code name – had been left in charge of operations in the secret room at the back of the house.

Mathilde was a young woman who had come from the Loire, ostensibly as a relation of the Parterres. She was a rather nervous, tense-looking young woman whose credentials for the job Dora had at first questioned. However there was no doubt as to her reliability or her patriotism. She had received no formal training but had impeccable references from the Loire circuit for whom she had acted as a courier. She also showed an aptitude for the work, a quick facility for mastering the codes and a steadiness in sending and receiving messages.

Dora felt however that, although self-effacing to the point of embarrassment, Mathilde was an obtrusive presence in the house and she would be glad when she left.

Soon she would move north to where the Allied landings were expected to take place, if they ever did. Some said it would be Normandy, some the Pas de Calais. So far they had had no warning as it was too risky.

Dora parked the car in the barn – petrol was so scarce that it could only be used a few times a month – and made her way through the inky blackness to the house. She thought how strange it was that one got so used to danger one almost no longer felt afraid. There was usually a chill, a frisson of fear on waking in the morning and then, with the normal events of the day taking their course, it disappeared, though there were sometimes many surreptitious comings and goings of people not connected with the wine business. Inevitably word had got round that Jean was considered 'hot' by the authorities, though no one could ever catch him doing anything he shouldn't be doing other than tending his vines.

This perpetual sense of danger had helped to bring husband and wife closer together. At one time, before the war, there had been an estrangement but Jean regarded her return to France in wartime, when she could have remained safely in England, not only heroic but as a true mark of devotion, a strengthening of the bonds of their marriage.

The house was always locked up, especially when an important clandestine meeting was taking place, and Dora, shivering with cold, was about to put her key in the lock of the back door with the aid of her torch when, to her surprise, it swung open. Inspecting the lock she saw that it had been broken. The kitchen was a large, comfortable traditional French kitchen where they usually ate, and where Jean had his meetings. With a mounting feeling of foreboding Dora crossed the floor and tried to switch on the lights but there was no electricity. Looking around for matches to light candles she was startled to see a beam of light in the corridor leading to the kitchen and, as it grew bigger, she put her hand to her mouth. From the beam of her own torch she was able now to see that that disorder prevailed in the room, as though there had been a fight.

"Jean . . ." she began shining her own torch in the direction of the beam. But no, it was not Jean. He would have said something, uttered a reassuring greeting.

Then a voice said tremulously, "Dora, it's me, Mathilde."

"Mathilde!" Dora exclaimed. "What has happened? Where are the others?"

"Oh, Dora!" Mathilde flung herself against her breast and Dora could feel tears on her face. "The Gestapo have been. They took everyone away. Oh, Dora you must *flee*. You must go at once. I am sure they will be back. They went everywhere looking for you. They said that they knew you were a British spy and they should have arrested you a long time ago."

"My God!" Dora abruptly sat down and stared at the beam of light on the floor. "There is no electricity."

"They cut the wires, the telephone. They broke open the door, ten or twelve of them, after surrounding the place."

"How long ago was this?" Dora felt as though an icy hand was clutching at her heart.

"An hour, two hours, I don't know. After dark. I was just bringing the men some coffee. They broke in and took them outside, bundled them straight into a van and drove away. There were about six of them, including Jean."

"All the leaders of the Resistance in the area," Dora said woodenly. Then, looking at the frightened face of her companion, "Did they find the wireless?"

"Oh yes. They broke down the door and took it away."

"And the codes?"

"Everything that was there they took."

Dora gently detached herself from Mathilde who had gradually recovered her self-possession, and walked slowly around the kitchen. There were a few pages of blank paper on the floor – difficult to tell how far the meeting had progressed – some broken glasses, an empty packet of cigarettes. Several of the chairs lay on their backs.

"They had no chance," she said turning to Mathilde who now sat dejectedly on one of the chairs.

"No chance!" Mathilde shook her head.

Dora's eyes narrowed and she looked speculatively at her companion. "*If* they took the men and the wireless. *If* everything was so well prepared, and clearly it was," Dora advanced slowly towards her. "If . . ." Suddenly she shone the beam of her torch right into Mathilde's face catching her unawares. Mathilde's eyes widened and she put up a hand to shade them from the glare as Dora continued, "*If* they took the men *and* the wireless, *if* they ransacked the house and searched everywhere for *me*," Dora's voice dropped almost to a whisper, "why didn't they take *you*?"

Mathilde opened her mouth and then closed it again, her mind clearly working furiously for an explanation. Suddenly the sound of a car outside broke the tension and before they could take shelter the back door was pushed open and the beam of another torch, this time a powerful one, stabbed the darkness. From the glow Dora could see the bearded face of Gregor the leader of a *réseau* south of the Marne.

"Dora, are you all right?"

Dora nodded still numbed by the realisation of her suspicion, apparently now justified, of a woman she had never really liked or trusted. Why had she not obeyed that instinct in the first place to send her away?

But Gregor was saying urgently, "We must get you out of here at once, Dora. You must leave immediately. No packing, nothing. They have taken Jean and the others to Gestapo Headquarters."

"And why didn't they take Mathilde?" Dora swung her torch over in her direction. "I was just asking her. She is our new wireless operator. She has only been here a short time. Logically, therefore, it must have been Mathilde who betrayed them."

Both Gregor and Dora now fastened their eyes on Mathilde who had her head in her hands. Gregor drew from his pocket a small snub-nosed pistol which he pointed at the cowering girl.

"Please, please," she pleaded raising her head, tears once again pouring down her cheeks. "They forced me to do it. They have arrested my fiancé. They said they would shoot him if I didn't turn Jean over to them. They had suspected his importance in the Resistance, the existence of the wireless, but they wanted proof. I am so sorry, so sorry."

"You think that will save your boyfriend, or *you*, you silly bitch?" Gregor clicked the safety catch off. "When people are dying every day for their country does it mean nothing to you to betray a whole circuit? Here," he pointed to Dora, "is an Englishwoman who has given up the safety of her country to serve France and the cause of freedom. Are you not ashamed to be in her presence?"

As he took careful aim, Dora seized his arm.

"No, please, Gregor," she cried. "There is enough bloodshed. I forbid it."

"Of what use is her life?" Gregor snarled brushing Dora's hand aside. "You think they will let her go? She is as good as dead, anyway. They will have no further use for her now." He raised his weapon and aimed it but Dora once more deflected his arm. "I say *no*, Gregor. I say *no!*"

"Very well." Gregor shrugged and put his gun back in his pocket. "Let her scrape a living from the earth like the beasts. She will be a fugitive. Her life is not worth living anyway. There is no hiding place for people like her."

Still trembling with fear Mathilde continued to gaze at the floor. Gregor took Dora by the arm and bundled her out of the door.

"Quickly, we have no time. We have a plane landing in a few hours and I think we can get you on it."

Dora looked back towards the house which she loved. "Can't I pack just a few things?"

"Nothing, nothing," Gregor insisted propelling her towards the car and pushing her into the back seat. "There is not a moment to lose." He glanced back at the house. "And with that little traitor, since you made me spare her miserable life, we have even less time."

"There is no telephone and she can't drive," Dora said. "Even if she does want to betray me, which I now doubt, she will have her work cut out to make contact with anyone before dawn. But, Gregor I am so worried about the animals. Who will feed them?"

"I will see to everything once you are on the plane. We have also to try and devise a plan to rescue Jean and the others before they are sent to Paris."

Gregor started the engine of the aged Citroën which gave a worrying cough before it spluttered into life. "By that time you'll be in England," he turned to Dora and gave a grim smile, "if all goes well."

Part Two

The Turning of the Tide

1944–1947

Nine

March 1944

Connie, hands deep in her pockets, wandered disconsolately around St Mark's Square occasionally dropping a few crumbs that she had in her pockets for the pigeons who, like the rest of the population, were hungry. It was a blustery day and the waters from the lagoon had overflowed the piazza forming a thin film about an inch deep, an occurrence which was becoming more frequent. One day the whole of Venice might be under water and all its treasures lost.

It seemed a horror not to be contemplated, and yet in comparison to the horrors of war what was the loss of a city, even an immortal one like Venice?

After the German occupation all the Jews had been rounded up and deported. Everywhere there was an atmosphere of fear. People were frightened. More than ever Connie, alone now after Paolo's death, felt she wanted to be gone.

News of the war trickled slowly into the city. The propaganda which came over the Nazi-controlled wireless was ignored. Those who were able crouched over their radio sets, the volume very low, to try and catch the voice of Radio Free Europe.

In January a massive Allied force had landed in Anzio, south of Rome, with the object of pressing on towards the capital, but it had met stiff resistance from the German army which still controlled the northern part of Italy, including Venice. Fierce fighting had centred on the town of Cassino and its beautiful and historic monastery was under attack.

Acting on the advice of Doctor Fattorino, Connie hardly ever left the palazzo except, after his death, to accompany Paolo's body to the Island of San Michele for burial. It had been a sad but brief farewell with only a handful of mourners. Fearful of arousing the interest of the authorities there had been no Mass but merely a committal and blessing from the parish priest, Father Giuseppe. Connie had returned to the palazzo with the few mourners who had attended the ceremony, close childhood friends of Paolo, as well as Doctor Fattorino and Father Giuseppe.

It was then that she had realised how few of Paolo's friends she really knew despite the number of years she'd lived in Italy, both on her own and as his wife.

The outbreak of war had seen the dispersal of most of the English community in Venice. When Italy had, not unexpectedly, entered the war on the side of Germany she had discovered that many of Paolo's friends with their Fascist tendencies had approved. Like him, they were all monarchists, Roman Catholics and, at first anyway, had considered that Mussolini was good for Italy.

Even with his fall and the collapse of Italy some of them hadn't changed. Connie found that she had nothing in common with them, and a stiff formality prevailed. After the reception following the funeral few had hung about and she had seen none of them since.

Thus she was condemned to a solitary existence made worse by worry about the war and the possible fate of her family from whom, inevitably, she had heard nothing.

There were few people in the piazza nowadays, certainly no tourists, and those who lingered were often objects of suspicion. From the corner of her eye she saw a man who seemed to be watching her and, trying not to show her fear by walking too quickly, she disposed of the rest of her crumbs and, as a flock of pigeons swooped on them, exited through one of the arches in the piazza to lose herself in the maze of narrow side streets surrounding it.

Once out of the square she walked quickly in the direction of the Rialto Bridge. Once or twice she slowed down, ostensibly to gaze into a shop window, when she would take a sideways glance in the direction she'd come, but there was no sign of anyone following her.

Connie finally arrived, a little breathless and with a renewed sense of fear, at the Palazzo Colomb-Paravacini and let herself in. She still had her maid Elena and an ancient family retainer of Paolo's, Francisco, and between them they looked after her. She and Paolo had long ago shut off more than half of the palazzo so as to give the servants less work. She now more or less lived in two rooms, her bedroom and a small salon which she used as a sitting room. All the large rooms were closed, the furniture covered with sheets. One had been opened for the funeral reception but as soon as the guests had departed the covers had been put on again and the doors locked.

Connie was surprised to see a coat on one of the chairs in the hall with a man's hat on top. As she divested herself of her own coat and hat and fluffed out her hair after a brief glance in the hall mirror, Francisco appeared and jerked his head towards the door of her sitting room.

"You have a visitor Contessa. Conte Giacomo Colomb-Paravacini."

"Oh!" Connie exclaimed in surprise when the door opened and Paolo's son stood looking at her.

She had only met him a handful of times: once when he was still a schoolboy staying with his father during the holidays, and the few occasions after their marriage when he had come to visit his father. Giacomo was now in his thirties, married and the father of three children. He and his sister had never made a secret of the fact that they did not approve of her, not so much because she had taken the place of their mother (who had died quite young) but because she was a Protestant and a divorced woman, and because of this they thought their father should not have married her.

As Connie walked towards him Giacomo greeted her formally with a little bow as he stretched out his hand.

"I am sorry to have called on you like this without an announcement," he said. "But you know it is very difficult to cross Italy now, especially as the Allied troops are advancing towards Rome."

"Do sit down, Giacomo." Connie, addressing him in Italian, pointed to a chair. "May I offer you some refreshment?"

Giacomo shrugged.

"I don't suppose you have whisky?"

"Oh, I think we have whisky." Connie looked at Francisco who hovered at the door.

"Whisky for the Count please and I will have coffee."

Francisco bowed and withdrew.

Giacomo, instead of accepting a seat, had crossed the room and stood by the window gazing across the canal for some time smoking a cigarette. Looking at him it was quite easy to imagine Paolo when young. Giacomo was tall, blond, urbane and quite handsome. He wore a double-breasted grey striped suit and two-tone brown and white shoes. There was, however, something about him that Paolo most definitely had not had: a shifty, rather mean expression, a way of avoiding looking directly into the eyes of the person he was addressing. Now, as he turned, his gaze was not on Connie but on some object on the far side of the room.

"I am very sorry I couldn't attend my father's funeral. My sister too. It was impossible for us to get permission to leave Rome in so short a time. I still have my duties at the Ministry of the Interior and it would have been unwise for me to ask for leave."

"Unwise?" Connie raised an eyebrow.

"To have drawn the attention of the Germans to father's death."

"But your father was a perfectly respectable, law-abiding

member of Venetian society. He hardly belonged to the criminal classes."

"However . . ." Giacomo shuffled his feet. "If I want to keep my job I have to toe the line."

"And that means kowtowing to the Germans?" Connie's lip curled with contempt.

"They are the occupying power," Giacomo replied haughtily. "They call the shots. I have a wife and family to support. I cannot single-handedly defy the occupying authorities, however much I might wish to do so."

"I suppose what you did not wish was to draw their attention to the fact that your father had an English wife?"

"Something like that." Giacomo nodded, pointedly examining his well-manicured nails. "I always thought my father made a mistake. My mother was of the noble Da Biondi-Leoni family – she was a *principessa* . . ." Giacomo with an expressive shrug of the shoulders, stared down his nose at Connie and she had great difficulty resisting the urge to slap his face.

Instead she said coldly, "Perhaps you would be kind enough to tell me why you are here other than to insult me? In other words please state your business and be gone."

"Certainly." Giacomo extinguished his cigarette, sat down and crossed his legs. "You may not realise, Contessa – I am not sure how much my father told you – but the Palazzo Colomb-Paravacini is entailed to the eldest son of the family." He paused and gazed around him, "This all belongs to me. The lawyers have been in touch with me and told me of my legal rights. I know that, to everyone's surprise, my father left very little money, but I also understand you are a woman not without means – maybe that is why he married you – and that you have, or had, your own residence on the other side of the canal, so this I'm sure will cause you no hardship or distress."

Connie swallowed. "I sold my Venetian residence when I married your father. To find another home at this stage will not be easy. It is also a slur on me, and your father, to say he married me for my money. As far as I know he had ample means for us both." She bit her lip. "As it happens money was something we never discussed. Somehow it didn't seem to us to be necessary. We had what we wanted and before the war could live well. Now, well," she shrugged, "we were in the same boat as everyone else. As his lawyers were in Rome I have not been in touch with them since his death, or they with me."

"No, but they were in touch with me. Perhaps my father was not completely honest with you, I don't know." Giacomo frowned. "Most of his fortune came from my mother the Principessa Magdalena Da Biondi-Leoni. When she died her fortune was divided between me and my sister. I think there was some small allowance for my father. However he is dead now and that no longer applies. The question is, what to do about you?" Giacomo produced his silver case and selected a fresh cigarette. "It is not impossible, I think, for you to find a suitable property. Many people, reduced to various states of poverty by the war, anxious to get their hands on some money, will be prepared to sell."

"But I am not in a position to buy. The bulk of my fortune remains invested in England."

"How unfortunate." Giacomo gave a silky smile. "But how wise. However, in that case I am prepared to be generous. I will give you four weeks' notice from today, and if you have not vacated my palazzo by that date I shall inform the authorities who might be very interested to know of your existence.

"The war is not over yet you know Contessa, and I am not at all sure that the Allies, who are still being held down at Cassino, will ultimately be victorious."

Guido and Francesca Valenti had been friends of Connie for over thirty years. Guido, a lawyer, had administered the estate of Connie's guardian Miss Fairchild of which Connie was the sole heir. Francesca, a blonde, worldly, sophisticated woman of great presence, vivacity and charm, had helped to transform the rather nervous, intensely shy young woman from a duckling into a swan. She had given her poise, confidence, a taste for fashion, helped her to make the best of her appearance, and introduced her into the élite cultural society of Venice.

During the years that Connie was married to Carson Woodville they had inevitably lost touch, but the friendship remained and had resumed, in fact had become even stronger, when Connie returned and settled in Venice.

The Valentis had a comfortable apartment off the Riva Degli Schiavoni, Venice's waterfront. It was full of old books and artistic treasures. They were opera buffs and had frequently taken Connie to La Fenice. During the war they continued to meet but less often. Connie had never dared ask, but she had an idea that, despite his age – he was over sixty – Guido was somehow connected with the Italian partisans who had opposed Mussolini. The Valentis had always had very left-wing views which had put them in conflict with Paolo.

Guido had come up from his office on a lower floor and sat listening to Connie describing the visit of her stepson. He said nothing but smoked a cigarette, looking out of the window, waiting until she had finished.

"Works for the Interior Ministry does he? I wonder in what capacity?" He looked across at Connie who shook her head.

"I've no idea."

"Maybe he helped to get all the Jews deported from Rome. Sounds like the sort of chap who might. Well," Guido's expression was one of grim satisfaction, "his turn will come. Meanwhile . . . we must get you out of Venice, Connie, as soon as we can. I don't trust your stepson for a moment."

"Then you think I have no rights to the palazzo?"

Guido shrugged. "I can't say anything about that until I have seen Paolo's will – if he left one. I suppose he did?"

Connie shook her head. "I've no idea."

"He never discussed it with you?"

"Never."

"I find that rather odd."

"Some people are afraid of death. Paolo didn't want to think about it. I never thought much about the future either, I must confess. We had sufficient for everything we wanted. Lately we wanted very little. We couldn't travel or indulge in any luxuries because of the war. We lived quite frugally. Although Paolo was seventy-five, when he died it was unexpected. If Giacomo says the estate is entailed I'm sure it is. He implied Paolo married me for my money, which I don't believe."

"Neither do I." Francesca, who had been listening intently, shook her head. "It is rubbish to suggest it."

"I knew nothing of his affairs," Guido concurred, "but I always understood he was well off."

"Giacomo implied it was his first wife's money."

"Maybe." Guido's expression was non-committal. "What does it matter? He is dead now and you are well off. You can do without his palazzo. I mean, I'm sure it has a sentimental value, but as long as this war continues we are helpless. When it is over I will pursue it as vigorously as I can to establish your rights." Guido lit another cigarette and got up. "However, that is not the point. You are in danger here. If you were not before, as Paolo's wife, you are now. His son, it seems, is in league with the Germans."

"We don't know for sure."

"We can be pretty sure if he is still with the Ministry of the Interior. It sounds to me as though he's very thick with them. Never mind. We shall get him after the war, along with all the others."

"*We?*" Connie looked hesitantly at him.

"Don't ask." Francesca gave her a warning look. "Just do as he advises."

"Then where can I go?" Connie felt the fear, the emptiness returning. "Can I get out of the country?"

"With difficulty, but it can be done. The trouble is that the Fascists are very strong in the mountains. The passes into France are too dangerous. Switzerland is a possibility, but it too has hazards because the Fascists are thick there too and they are supported by many of the Swiss. I can get you on a boat out of Venice but the seas are dangerous and Greece and Yugoslavia are enemy occupied. An aeroplane is quite out of the question." Guido leaned thoughtfully across a table and frowned. "Frankly I'm a bit stumped. I think the best thing is to head for the mainland and put you in a safe house."

"A safe house!" Connie suddenly brightened. "I have a safe house."

"You have a safe house? Where?"

"Alexander, Carson's son – of whom I am very fond and who I think is fond of me – has a house on Como. It will have been closed all during the war."

"You know where it is?"

"Of course I know where it is. I visited it several times. Alexander was not often there but allowed Paolo and me to go whenever we wished."

Guido still didn't look happy.

"Como is just in the area where Mussolini hangs out. It could be even more dangerous than here. The house, if it was empty, might have been requisitioned. Does Giacomo know about this house?"

"Oh, no, he knows nothing at all. During my marriage to Paolo I only met him a few times. Father and son were not close and he was never very friendly. He did not like me."

"So it seems." Guido ground out his cigarette. "Well we shall have to chance it. I will ask our people there to find out more before we send you."

"And will it take long?"

"It will take as long as a bird flies. I cannot use the telephone but we have other means just as swift." Guido smiled mysteriously.

"But how . . . ?" Connie began but Francesca leaned forward and took her hand.

"I told you not to ask," she said caressing Connie's cheek gently. "The less you know the better for you. Believe me."

May 1944

The tide had finally turned in favour of the Allies and from all the theatres of war the stories were of the enemy on the run. In Russia, the Red Army had fought its way through to the Crimea all the time thrusting back the Germans. American forces in the Pacific made new conquests against the Japanese. In Italy the Allies continued their slow advance towards Rome, fiercely resisted by the Germans, and throughout occupied Europe there were sporadic mutinies and bursts of rebellion and unrest led by the resistance movements.

Alexander, on short home leave from Italy where he had been supporting Allied troops from the air, had collected Minnie and driven her down to Forest House where Lally had offered them the cottage on the estate where she could rest and, if she desired, have her baby.

Alexander had been very reluctant to let Minnie stay in London where he had lost Mary in childbirth. In his inevitable absence having Lally and the family near meant that they would keep an eye on Minnie. He had no idea in what theatre of war he would be when the time came.

Minnie and Alexander arrived in time for lunch and were delighted to find that Carson and Dora were also there. Sally had decided to stay behind because of a cold.

It was a joyful reunion between Dora and Alexander who had not met since her return to England, after a dangerous aircraft journey ducking the flack of enemy fire. Carson too was delighted to see his son – an air ace, a war hero. As a military man and himself decorated in the first war, Carson was very proud of him.

Minnie, five months pregnant, had left the WAAF which had no place for pregnant women, married or unmarried. The idea of living in the country close to Alexander's family had at first filled her with some doubt. She liked being in London, near to her friends, where Alexander was able to slip home on short leave. She felt that in Dorset she had, understandably, to share him with the rest of his family, and to her her time with him was precious: there were too many imponderables, both as regards the war and its aftermath.

"The cottage is very tiny," Lally said apprehensively as they sat in the drawing room after lunch drinking ersatz coffee. "It was meant for the servants. In those days, of course we had far more than we do now."

"It is a lovely cottage," Carson said expansively blowing smoke from one of his precious, pre-war cigars into the air. He was delighted to have his family around him: his son, and his cousin to whom he had always been close. It was through him that Dora had met and subsequently married Jean Parterre. Carson turned to Lally and smiled. "What others might not know, Lally, is that I lived there for some time."

"*You* lived there Father? I didn't know that." Alexander looked at him in surprise.

"After my father married Agnes." Carson paused as if the reason was difficult to explain. "Well, she and I never got on, so I moved out of Pelham's Oak." He gazed fondly at his son. "It is also here that you, as a small boy, were staying with Lally and I had the first inklings that you and I were related."

"How did you know that, Father?"

"Because you so resembled your mother, and then Lally produced the bombshell that you had been abandoned and left on her doorstep. Of course there was no proof, and nothing I could do about it then. I used to play with you. Do you remember, Lally?"

"I remember." Lally drained her cup. "And I remember how fond little Alexander was of you and you of him. You seemed to have a strange bond even then." She looked wistfully out of the window. "See, the sun has come out. Why don't we go and take a look before it starts to rain again?"

They all rose and trooped out of the French windows across the terrace and round the house in the direction of the thatched cottage which had been converted from stables at the time the main house was built. It was a low two-storey building set among trees with a paved courtyard where, at one time, the horses had gathered before the meet. But Lally disapproved of fox-hunting and banned it after Prosper's death. Now the horses were for riding only and comfortably housed in new stables a short distance away.

Minnie looked with excitement, but also with some apprehension, at the cottage which, for the foreseeable future, was to be her home. It was indeed very pretty in its attractive rural setting with rambling roses across the front walls in bud and purple clematis in full flower. One of the upstairs windows was open, and the sun, which now shone quite strongly, cast a dappled effect on the warm sandstone walls. She clutched Alexander's hand and smiled.

"Happy?" he whispered.

"Ecstatically," she whispered back. "It's like a dream home."

"It is yours," Lally said noticing their glances, "for as long as you wish." She waved a hand airily around her. "I mean this whole place. Everything comes to Alexander when I die so, in a sense, it is yours already."

"But Alexander and I aren't . . . ." Minnie bit her lip. There was always that uncertainty, that threat of something happening to spoil their love as the return of Irene undoubtedly would. It was like a cloud perpetually hovering over them and somehow it seemed so unworthy to hope that she might not return. So every time one thought about the future hope was tinged with guilt, expectation with remorse.

Dora hung back, reluctant to enter the cottage. Her father had fallen from the roof while he had been thatching it and been killed. This was why her mother had not wanted to join today's party. They both knew it was foolish. It had happened a very long time ago – nearly fifty years – and yet throughout that time they both avoided going into the cottage or anywhere near it whenever they visited Lally.

Indeed the servants had always refused to live there. They regarded it as unhappy, a legend which had stuck, which was why it remained empty.

Carson turned round and looked at Dora as the young couple disappeared inside, followed by Lally.

"Come in," he said putting out his hand.

"You know why I don't like going inside . . ."

"Of course I know." He kept his hand out. "And it's silly. If you don't go inside the young couple will wonder why, and if you tell them it might spoil their day."

Dora looked at him, resolutely squared her shoulders and smiled.

"Time to banish ghosts," she said and, her hand tightly gripping Carson's, she crossed the threshold into the main room where Minnie was already uttering cries of joy. Lally had completely redecorated and furnished the cottage. The furniture and curtains were new. Everywhere there were flowers, rugs on the highly polished wooden floors, and a great fire roaring up the chimney. They tramped upstairs to find the same care had been taken to plan for the comfort and happiness of the lovers. In the main bedroom Lally had added an *en suite* bathroom. There was a large double bed with a white cretonne bedspread, heavy thick Wilton carpet on the floor and a bowl of spring flowers on the polished table by the window, on either side of which were large easy chairs.

"It is *perfect*," Minnie cried bouncing on the bed, patting it for Alexander to come and sit beside her.

"Perfect." His hand closed over hers. Then, he said, looking at Lally, "You have taken an awful lot of trouble over this, Mother."

Lally looked pleased. "I'm so glad you like it. And next to you . . ." Lally threw open a communicating door with a flourish, "is the nursery, which I have had specially converted."

They all trooped into the room which was decorated in a pale-yellow with oval cartoon-like paintings of ducks, kittens and rabbits decorating the walls. There were yellow curtains, a soft cream carpet, and a wicker crib covered with a cretonne hood, resting on rockers so that the baby could gently be lulled to sleep. There was a large white dresser, a table and low chairs.

"And next door is the nanny's room," Lally continued with the same note of pleasurable excitement, leading the way out of the nursery and into a room which had a single bed, a chest of drawers, dressing table and the same cream carpet as the nursery.

"It is absolutely heaven, Lally," Alexander said, kissing her.

"It's *really* beautiful." Minnie seemed almost close to tears. "You've been so good to us, Lally."

"And I will be here, my dear," Lally put an arm round her waist drawing her close, "to see that you are well looked after, as well as I can until Alexander returns, and then you can have this as your own little country cottage, your very own, to come to whenever you wish."

For the first part of their journey back to Pelham's Oak Carson and Dora remained silent, each locked in their own thoughts. It was not difficult to guess what they might be.

The war was coming to an end – the Allied invasion of Europe was expected soon as activity was increasing on the south coast and certain areas had been made out of bounds to the public. Armoured carriers rumbled unceasingly through the quiet country lanes.

Dora had not heard from Jean since she had left France and the authorities in London had had no word of his fate or that of his comrades captured on the same night. No word at all either had been heard from Irene or Bart since their disappearance. If the end of the war brought peace, what unwelcome revelations might it not also bring? Carson and Dora seemed to be sharing the same line of thought.

"It is dreadful to hope that Irene will not come back," Dora said at last settling back and lighting a cigarette. She looked at Carson whose expression remained grave. "But I'm afraid I do hope it. I must. Minnie and Alexander are so idyllically happy, so well suited, and there's a baby on the way. It is very difficult not to believe that, in many ways, Alexander might not wish that too."

"If Irene *does* come back," Carson changed gear to go up the steep hill leading to Pelham's Oak, "and I think it most unlikely that she will – I'm afraid she has perished in a concentration camp – then she and Alexander will have to reassess the situation, as a lot of other couples will have to. Owing to the pressures of war many new relationships will have been formed. No one, certainly not Irene, can expect things to be as they were in 1939."

"You think then that they will divorce?"

"I think it is inevitable. Alexander will have fathered a child by Minnie; they will have created a new family together. It is hard not to think that, after so many years, Irene will not be able to accept and understand this. But," Carson braked as they approached the portico of the house, 'I don't think it will happen and when Alexander does trace her, if ever he does, and discovers what happened to her, then he will be free."

As Carson got out of the car and went round to open the door for Dora, David the butler came solemnly down the stairs, his expression impassive as usual.

He assisted Dora from the car, gave a bleak smile and then said, "There is someone to see you, Mrs Parterre."

"Oh?" Momentarily Dora's face lit up with expectation.

"It is a lady, madam. From London." The butler then got into the driving seat and drove the car round to the garage and out of sight of the house.

Carson took Dora's arm as they mounted the steps.

"I wonder who it can be?" Carson murmured. "I do hope they don't want you to return to France."

"If they do I shall go," Dora said and her expression turned to a smile as she saw Madame Greuz emerge from the drawing room and walk slowly towards her. Behind her stood Sally, pale-faced, but that might have been because she was still suffering from a heavy cold.

"Madame Greuz!" Dora exclaimed clasping her hand, her eyes lighting up, and breaking into French. "Marie, it is very good to see you again." During her training she and the Frenchwoman had become firm friends.

"And you, Dora." Marie Greuz held on to Dora's hand looking intently at her. Dora's face froze. Madame Greuz led her into the drawing room while Carson and Sally remained outside.

"You've something to tell me about Jean?" As they stopped Dora stared at her visitor who was still clasping her hand.

Marie nodded, searching for words.

"It is not good news?" Dora prompted her.

"Jean, our dear 'Gabriel', is dead, Dora." Marie's eyes were stricken. "Oh, I am so sorry to give you the news. Believe me . . ." She appeared on the verge of breaking down herself.

Dora clung onto her hand aware that Carson and Sally had silently entered the room and were standing supportively behind her.

"He died a hero, Dora, a hero of France, of the free world."

Dora felt Carson's hand on her shoulder as he tried to draw her gently down onto the sofa, but she resisted him.

"How . . ." she began tremulously, "when?"

"It was very soon after he was captured. He and the others were taken out and shot after a cruel interrogation during which they were tortured. However, none of them released any information, or gave away any secrets which is why it has taken us so long to discover their fate. They held firm, betraying no one. I wanted to come personally to tell you the terrible news."

"No possibility . . . of a mistake?" Dora whispered aware that she was clutching at straws.

Marie Greuz shook her head.

"I'm afraid none at all. The bodies were found, correctly identified, and given a decent burial. I hope that will be of some small comfort to you."

"Very small," Dora said bending her head. "Very small indeed."

Suddenly she felt bitter and looked defiantly, her eyes full of pain, towards her colleague, Carson and Sally. "I don't know how I shall face the world without Jean, knowing I am never going to see him again. I suppose I will. I must."

She seemed to make a supreme, conscious effort to take control of herself, to disport herself as Jean, brave Jean, who gave no secrets away, would have wanted her to. "I must go quickly to tell Louise before anyone else does." She embraced her friend whose eyes, now brimming with tears, followed her as she left the room.

"It is always sad to bring news like this," Marie said addressing no one in particular. "But especially sad because I became so fond of Dora and such an admirer of Jean Parterre, or 'Gabriel' to give him the code name by which we best knew him, though I never met him. He was a great leader. His name will never be forgotten." She gave a wan smile and looked at the two grief-stricken people in front of her. "Some small comfort. No? It is much better to live, but with honour. And Gabriel would never have done a dishonourable thing."

"It is inconceivable," Carson agreed seizing her hand. "And thank you for coming personally with the news. As well as being my cherished cousin's husband he was my friend for many years, a man I loved – a great man who, as you say, died as he lived: with honour."

Ten

May 1944

As Deborah stood on the docks watching the body of men at work all around her there was such an air of excited anticipation that it was impossible not to be swept away by it. Her workforce had swelled as the orders poured in from the army in preparation for the invasion of Europe which she knew was imminent. She was able to come and go freely, but some of the men were not going to be allowed to leave the site until the invasion had started.

It was rumoured that spies were everywhere. She had been sworn not to talk about what she saw, or where she had been, or discuss it with anyone, that is except her partner, her brother-in-law Abel Yetman.

He was somewhere on the huge artificial harbour which was being constructed and which would be towed by tugs over to France and would be large enough to service ships of up to 10,000 tons. Deborah shivered and pulled her coat tightly around her. The weather was crucial to the success of the landings and, so far, the outlook wasn't good.

It was late afternoon and she looked round for Abel. With only petrol enough for one car she was dependent on him for a lift back. Abel was in his element. Debarred from serving in the war, as he wished, he now found himself playing a useful, even a vital part in designing the huge reinforced concrete caissons whose assembly would constitute a truly remarkable artificial harbour, of crucial importance to the ships servicing the attacking forces.

Abel was a cheerful, robust, hardworking man, God-fearing and upright, who had been only eight at the time of his father's suicide. He had two younger sisters and thus grew up very quickly, becoming the man of the family, and a great support and consolation to his mother. He had left school early to be apprenticed to a builder and had started a business which had been successful until Bart Sadler became involved with it. After that, Abel found himself out on a limb and life, from being even tenored and uneventful, had became complicated. He had flung himself into odd jobs, but wartime had made these harder to find and when his sister-in-law had sought his help in reactivating Bart's business – with the added advantage that Bart wasn't there – he had been only too happy to agree, despite the fact that the very last person Abel had ever expected to be in business with was Deborah. Yet she had proved herself adept at it and eager to succeed. She was clever with figures, well organised, a woman with brains and skills in what was very much a man's world.

Their partnership had prospered. Deborah ran the office and saw to the paperwork, Abel was the link man with the clients. He assessed the jobs and prepared estimates. He was very experienced and knew what he was talking about. Then he would oversee the supplies, the workforce and the carrying out of the work.

Pretty soon Deborah realised that she would never have got anywhere without Abel's knowledge and expertise which was much much greater than Sam's.

Against all expectations Sam had recovered enough to be recalled to active service, which was what he wanted, and the business was now wholly in the hands of Deborah and Abel, that is until Bart got back or Sam returned from the war, whichever happened first. Then there would be a radical reappraisal, possibly another cataclysmic change that neither liked to think about.

Suddenly there was a hoot behind her and she turned to

see Abel waving to her from the open tourer, the engine running.

"Hop in," he shouted, "or we'll be shut in for the night."

As he threw open the door of the passenger seat Deborah ran over and climbed in only just in time as he drove off towards one of the many security barriers that blocked their way to the final exit.

Once on the open road he stopped and lit a cigarette. His hands were grimy with oil and under his jacket he still had on a pair of greasy dungarees. He was a good-looking man with curly black hair and blue, short-sighted eyes for which he wore glasses. It was his eyesight that had let him down and made him a reject for military service.

"Nearly ready," he said with a deep sigh of satisfaction. "I wish I could go over with it."

"Might they let you?" Deborah looked surprised.

Abel shrugged. "I think they'll only have army engineers. But I may be in with a chance."

Impulsively Deborah put a hand on his arm.

"I do wish that, if they offer you the chance, you'll turn it down."

"But why?" Now it was Abel's turn to show surprise.

"Well . . ." Deborah struggled to find the right words. "I should hate anything to happen to you."

"I see." Abel stubbed out his cigarette, turned on the engine and drove on.

In 1930 he had married his cousin, Deborah's sister, Ruth Woodville. He had built them a fine house on land given to them by Carson and the happy pair had settled down in hopeful expectation of a family to cement their love. Abel saw himself as very much the family man. His roots were in Wenham and he wanted to continue the Yetman dynasty started by his great-great-grandfather Thomas, born in 1800, and a successful builder in Blandford.

However, the family had failed to materialise. Doctors had been consulted to no avail and Abel and Ruth, while trying to come to terms with the fact that they would be childless, nevertheless started to grow apart each becoming locked in their own ways of courting forgetfulness: Abel with his building business, Ruth in excessive attention to good works.

It had been very annoying to see Deborah, the black sheep of the family, an idler who had caused nothing but trouble, marry a wealthy man and prove herself more fruitful than her virtuous and hardworking sister, who had never in her life given her mother or anyone who cared for her a single sleepless night.

Nevertheless it was perhaps inevitable that Abel had come to find Deborah's cheerful, positive company preferable to her sister's who had turned into something of a nag, always pointing out Abel's faults to him and seeming to discover new ones every day. It was with a heavy heart that he would return to his home at night, dreading to hear the sound of that scolding voice almost before he had put his key in the door. What was more, Ruth did not pay as much attention to her looks as her sister who went at least once a week to the hairdresser and spent as much money as she could, and as coupons would allow, on clothes, and was a deft hand with make-up. Deborah, on the lookout, made the best of herself; Ruth, defeated and depressed, did not.

Abel felt a hand on his knee and looked sideways at Deborah.

"Wouldn't you miss me too?" Deborah asked. "I mean, if *I* went away wouldn't *you* be sad?"

Abel braked and brought the car to a halt in a lay-by off the main road. The wind had caught Deborah's cheeks and ruffled her hair. Her blue eyes sparkled and the tip of her pink tongue peeped enticingly through her sensuous, slightly parted lips.

As she leaned over he caught a sight of cleavage and her subtle but sensuous perfume wafted towards him.

"Wouldn't you be sad?" she repeated. *"Wouldn't* you?"

Abel took Deborah in his arms and crushed his lips against hers. He could feel tears on her cheeks and he licked them with his tongue like a cat grooming its kitten. His whole body cried out to merge with hers, as though they had been made for each other.

"Of course I would miss you," he murmured. "I adore you."

They embraced again. When they drew apart they each sat in silence as if contemplating the momentous nature of what had just happened. Then Abel put out his hand.

"You don't look very happy."

"I *am* happy," Deborah insisted vigorously brushing the tears away from her eyes. "But I am apprehensive too. Oh Abel, what on earth is going to become of us? What are we to do?"

She paused looking appealingly at him: the practised vamp of whom the family disapproved, of whom few had a good word to say, yet he knew he loved her . . . and, unlike Ruth, he also knew her to be sexually alive and, above all, fecund.

"We'll find a way," Abel said holding tightly to her hand. "I am never going to let you go."

September 1944

"A boy!" Lally exclaimed clasping her hands together. "Alexander will be so thrilled."

Sitting up in the bed of the nursing home in Dorchester holding her baby, Minnie looked pale but pretty, her dark hair fastened back with a large bow, a touch of rouge adding colour to her cheeks.

It was difficult to tell, at the age of a few hours, which parent the baby resembled as both were dark with brown eyes. The baby had quite a mop of thick black hair but at this early stage it was impossible to determine the colour of his eyes.

Alexander was still somewhere in Europe where the Germans were retreating on all fronts. Paris had fallen to the victorious Allies. A massive force, in which the Free French Army had played a leading part, had landed on the south coast of France. Belgium was free and in the east the Russians were advancing towards the west, the ultimate goal being Berlin.

Carson had driven Minnie to the nursing home when she began labour. He had waited as anxiously as any father while she gave birth, a comparatively easy affair only lasting a few hours. It was a very emotional moment when he held his first grandson in his arms, and even more emotional when, a few hours later, Sally arrived with Lally and they cooed over the latest addition to the family.

Eliza and Dora telephoned for news. A telegraph was sent to Minnie's parents in the Bahamas. Kate, now eleven, and at a convent boarding school in Devon was informed about the arrival of her baby brother. Perhaps she was a little jealous because she seemed in no hurry to rush home and see him.

Everyone in the family and beyond knew except the baby's father, now a Group Captain, but a message had been sent through the Air Ministry in London which, hopefully, would reach him.

It seemed that at a time like this, after five weary years of war and the terrible uncertainty it had induced, a new baby, a new life, brought a surge of hope and optimism.

However, ten days later when Carson drove Minnie home there was still no news from Alexander, and Minnie had begun to fret.

Lally wanted her to stay in Forest House where she could keep an eye on her, but Minnie felt that if Alexander should return unexpectedly he would go to the cottage, and it was there that she insisted on taking their child. Massie was installed in the room next door to the nursery.

For Massie it was a time of great joy to have charge of Nelly's grandson, and she drooled over him and fussed over his mother and sat watching them while Minnie fed the baby, or tried to feed him, for she had little milk. She also appeared to get thinner and Lally began to worry that Minnie, though more robust than Alexander's first wife, might go the way Mary had gone if he did not contact them soon.

So the baby's arrival was a time of mixed blessings – joy in a new life, worry about his mother, and the fear that his father might never see him.

Minnie had a maid called Tabitha who used to come over from the big house to look after her. She had always refused to sleep in the cottage, even before the baby was born and there was room for her. Minnie had never questioned her about this but now she was curious, as it would be useful to have Tabitha on the spot and not always to have to telephone across to the house for her.

"I don't know why you don't want to sleep here?" Minnie said to her one day as she was busy about the bedroom tidying and making the bed while Minnie sat at her dressing table making-up her face, trying to banish some of the pallor which she knew worried Lally. "I'm sure the attic, which is large, could be made into a bedroom for you. It's very cosy here. Massie is very happy. Until it's ready, you could sleep in Massie's room, there's space for another bed. Then you could take it in turns to get up if baby cries at night."

Tabitha said nothing but continued to smooth the sheets before drawing up the blankets and putting on the quilt.

"It isn't as though you've *always* lived in Forest House," Minnie continued. "Would you like me to ask Mrs Martyn about the attic? It's nice and big. Then we could all be cosy together."

"I'd rather stay where I am, madam," Tabitha replied primly completing her task and turning her attention to the wardrobe, sorting through Minnie's dresses, holding one up after the other. "What will you do with them now, madam? The ones you wore when you were expecting? Will you save them for the next?"

Tabitha looked at her archly.

Minnie smiled. "We shall have to see what happens, Tabitha. I must say I am anxious about the Group Captain. I can't understand why he has not been in touch with me. It makes me very uncertain and apprehensive about the future. But look, you didn't answer my question. I want to know why you don't want to sleep here? Now that I have the baby it would be so much more convenient, you could help Massie out a lot until I am stronger and able to get up at night myself."

"I can't say, madam." Tabitha who was normally a sensible, uncomplicated girl of nineteen, a farmer's daughter, hung her head.

"Is there something wrong with the cottage? Something you know?" Minnie demanded. "If so you must tell me."

"I was asked not to say, madam."

"Not to say *what*? By whom?" Minnie now began to feel seriously alarmed and spots of colour, unaided by make-up, appeared on her cheeks.

Tabitha who was usually of an open, sunny disposition continued to hang her head.

"I *insist* on knowing, Tabitha," Minnie said with a hard edge to her voice, "or else I shall go straight to Mrs Martyn and demand to know the answer."

"Well, madam," Tabitha's voice sank to a mere whisper, "they *do* say this cottage is haunted."

"Oh, what nonsense!" Minnie tossed her head back and laughed. "Is *that* all it is? Some silly country story I expect."

"Oh no, madam," Tabitha looked indignant. "It was Mrs Heering's first husband, Ryder Yetman, fell off the roof of this very building and was killed. They say *his* ghost haunts the house and there are people alive to this day who have seen it. They say it is an unlucky house and it is because of what happened to Mr Yetman when he broke his neck all those years ago."

That night Minnie woke in a sweat and lay in her bed her ears alert for sounds, not of the baby crying, or her heart thumping in her chest, but for the sound of ghostly footsteps: Ryder Yetman's uneasy spirit which had not yet found rest.

An unlucky house. That was the information that had bothered her more than the story of the ghost. They said that women who had just given birth were prey to melancholy and flights of fantasy, but supposing Ryder's ghost *did* walk there? Was it to warn her of unhappiness ahead? She knew that Eliza avoided visiting the cottage. She had seen Dora's reluctance to enter it on the day she first visited it, and now she knew why. This was something that had been deliberately kept from her.

She heard the sound of knocking and sat up, her heart still thumping.

"Come in," she cried and turned on the light. It was half past three and Massie's comfortable figure appeared round the door.

"What is it, Massie?" she cried. "Something wrong with the baby?"

"No, bless you, dearie," Massie said crossing to the bed. "It was you woke me with your screams, not him. I wondered if you was all right."

"Screams?" Minnie said wonderingly. "I didn't know. I must have had a bad dream." She felt her forehead which was hot and sticky, then realised her whole body was drenched in sweat and sank back on her bed, trembling. "Oh, Massie, what shall I do?"

"What ails you, madam? What worries you with that dear little baby safe by your side and everyone around to love and care for you?"

"We haven't heard from Alexander." Minnie took hold of Massie's hand and held on to it tightly. "Not a word in three weeks. If he had heard about the baby surely he would have contacted us? They say that this is an unlucky house. That it's haunted, and I have such dreadful foreboding that something awful has happened to Alexander, that he'll never know his son and I'll never see him again."

"Of *course* the house isn't haunted," Carson said robustly. "I lived here for many months and was very happy here."

Minnie was a little in awe of Carson. He was an impressive, almost towering figure and as he was Alexander's father she was anxious to make a good impression on him. Now she was annoying him with her childish fears. Alexander would not have been pleased.

They were sitting next to each other on the sofa in the sitting room of the cottage, careful to keep a sizeable gap between them.

"I didn't know Mrs Heering's first husband lost his life here. Tabitha said it is his ghost that walks."

Carson didn't try to conceal his irritation. The worry of the war, his responsibilities as commander of the local Home Guard and the death of Jean Parterre had taken their toll and his temper was short.

"Ryder Yetman's was an unfortunate accident. It doesn't make the place haunted. Ryder was too robust and sensible a man for that sort of nonsense. You can be sure he rests quietly in his grave up at the churchyard in Wenham. You know what servants can be like. They are sometimes very superstitious. I never saw any trace of Ryder Yetman's ghost, or ever had any indication that the cottage was anything but a good, safe place in which to live."

Carson's tone softened and he looked anxiously at Minnie.

"There is no need at all to be frightened, my dear, or if you are Lally would be only too glad to have you over at the house."

He made an awkward attempt to comfort her by putting a hand on her arm. The truth was that Minnie made him nervous too.

If she had been a legitimate daughter-in-law he would have known their respective roles. Now these were ill-defined. A proper sense of relationship was lacking. For instance, after the war there was nothing to stop her taking off with his grandson if she wished – without legal bonds, Alexander had no rights. The situation made Carson uncomfortable and he would dearly have loved it to be regularised.

Minnie, also uneasy with Alexander's father, appreciated his awkward gesture and brushed a lock of hair out of her eyes. "I know it's silly of me and . . . thank you, Sir Carson, for being so kind and understanding. You may think me a foolish woman, prey to unreasonable fears. It is just that . . . it is such a *long* time since we had news of Alexander. I am terribly afraid something might have happened to him."

"My dear." Carson moved closer and gently took her hand. He was by nature an affectionate man but nervous of being too demonstrative with Minnie in case she misunderstood him. "If something had happened to Alexander we should have heard. Make no mistake about that. Bad news travels very fast in wartime. I am sure that Alexander is in the thick of the action somewhere in Europe and that he is in good health and we shall soon be hearing from him again, if not seeing him. Because things are so different from the war in which I fought, I have really little idea of the conditions our men are fighting under. Communications are of the utmost importance so the wires cannot be clogged up with personal messages. Alexander may not yet know of the existence of the baby. He was a little premature, I understand, so he will not be worrying either. In times of war men cannot control their own lives or what they do. They are under orders at all times to obey. Believe me, if I thought anything was amiss I would tell you. But I have faith in Alexander. He is a great airman, a fine man, and I am proud of him." He shook her hand gently. "Now Minnie, you must be brave too. You are surrounded here by Alexander's family who love you as one of their own." He gazed steadily into her eyes. "Promise me no more tears? No more foolish fears?"

"I promise," Minnie said summoning a brave smile.

They went up to see the baby, chatted to Massie and then Minnie walked Carson to the front door. He kissed her tenderly on the cheek as he took his farewell and, with a wave, crossed the yard towards the house to see Lally.

Minnie watched him until he disappeared and then she turned towards the cottage again, but was reluctant to go in. Instead she walked round to the garden at the back and sat for a while staring at the roof from which Ryder Yetman had fallen, trying hard to imagine that scene over fifty years before when he had been thatching the roof and, for some reason, lost his footing and fell.

It had broken everyone's heart. He was such a well-loved and popular man. It had plunged his widow into near poverty and Julius, the man for whom the house had been built, had never wanted to live there.

Yet Lally had lived here for many, many years and Alexander had spent most of his youth here.

Of course it was silly servants' talk to say the place was haunted. Yet, all the same, as she looked at it, even though it was a day of bright sunshine, a shiver ran through her and in her bones she felt it was an unlucky place in which to live.

Alexander drove wearily through the night. His eyes were red with exhaustion, but this was a state he was quite used to. He didn't know how long it was since he had had a proper night's sleep. He was always on the alert for the call that would summon him to another operation in support of the bombers, or to attack the fleeing ranks of the enemy being driven back in Europe, as formerly occupied countries regained their independence.

He was desperate for news of Minnie and had begged forty-eight hours' leave which was well overdue anyway. For this reason, in order not to lose precious time, he drove through the night without stopping until he came to Forest House, its turrets just appearing above the trees in the dawn light.

Forest House. Home. He was a warrior accustomed to concealing emotion but, slowly, his eyes filled with tears and he angrily brushed them away, glad that none of the tough men under his command could see him. But what, in the same circumstances, might they not do after all? They had homes and families too.

There was something about home, as there was about the first sight of the green countryside of England after the parched, battle-scarred lands of continental Europe that never failed to move him.

So as not to disturb the people in the house or set the dogs barking Alexander left his car a quarter of a mile away and approached on foot, walking round it by a footpath through the woods to the cottage at the back which lay in semi-darkness.

Almost fearfully, now that he was here at last, he stood gazing at it. Then he produced his key and quietly let himself in.

Nothing stirred. Not a murmur. He wondered, for a moment, if anyone was there. Suddenly all the anxiety he'd felt about Minnie and her condition, which he had tried to suppress, surfaced and he raced up the stairs two at a time then stopped abruptly and listened. He heard it again: the cry of a baby. Simultaneously the door of Minnie's bedroom flew open and Minnie, hair tousled, clutching at her nightgown, stood in the doorway a look of terror on her face which changed rapidly, first to one of incredulity and then of joy when she saw who was standing at the top of the stairs. With a strangled cry she threw herself in his arms.

"Oh, Alexander I thought I would never see you again. And darling . . ." her face shining she stood back from him and looked at him, "we have a baby . . ."

"So I heard." Alexander's voice choked with emotion.

"Did you not know? Were you not told?"

"No."

"A boy . . ." Minnie pointed to where Massie had suddenly appeared in the doorway of the nursery with the baby in her arms. Slowly Alexander approached her, his hands outstretched. Then he took the infant, whose tears had stopped abruptly at the sight of a stranger, and cuddled him.

"What's his name?" he asked looking at Minnie.

"We waited for you. We call him 'Baby'."

"We'll have to change that." Alexander smiled and, for a long time, rested his cheek against his son's, his heart too full of emotion to speak as he silently gave thanks that his life had been spared to see him.

Eleven

April 1945

C onnie sat with her arms folded, shoulders hunched,
smoking furiously, head pressed close to the wireless
to catch the voices crackling over the receiver. At times the
reception was very poor but she knew that Mussolini was
dead, captured while trying to escape and, after a brief trial,
he had been shot with his mistress, Clara Petacci, at Dongo
not very far away from where she was now.

She had been hiding for so long, keeping to the shelter of the
villa, that she felt no urge to go out and welcome the soldiers
of the liberating forces with the rest of the population. Even
above the sound of the wireless she could hear the shouting in
the streets as wave after wave of excited citizens, young and
old, ran past waving the Italian flag high above their heads.

For a year Connie had remained in Alexander's villa seeing
hardly anybody except the maid, Luisa, who took care of it in
Alexander's absence, and who shopped and cleaned for her.
She had been very lucky to have her; otherwise she might be
dead. Solely dependent on the loyalty and goodwill of one
person Connie had nevertheless feared for her life as she knew
that the Fascist forces were concentrated in the north, where
Mussolini had been operating his 'Italian Socialist Republic'
from his hideaway in the mountains.

Almost Connie's sole preoccupation since her flight from
Venice had been to follow day by day, hour by hour the
progress of the war; the slow, agonisingly slow, advance of

149

the Allied forces through Italy. Day after day she had sat close
to her wireless, sometimes unable to hear the news because of
the static, terrified of discovery by the Germans or the Italian
Fascists holed up around the lake of Como. She had nothing
else to do. Occasionally she saw a paper brought in by Luisa.
There were a few books in the villa, all of which she had read
and reread, and some very old pre-war magazines.

There was no one to write to or, rather, no point in trying
because there was no post. She had no idea what had happened
or what was happening to her relatives in England, especially
her children who were now nearly grown up. She dreaded that
her sons might have enlisted in the war.

It was a lonely existence. In a way not an existence at all:
pecking at food, creeping around stealthily outside by night
sticking close to the villa walls in order to get some exercise,
cut off from human company except that of Luisa. Half the
time she wondered if she could be trusted, or if even she might
be prepared to betray her for money. In this atmosphere no one
could be relied on.

But Luisa hadn't. She had remained loyal and now the Germans had signed an unconditional surrender to the Americans
at Caserta. The war in Italy was over.

Was it safe to go out? Connie turned off the wireless and
looked longingly towards the door. Maybe soon, but not
yet. There were still pockets of the enemy roaming the
villages round Como, both sides, Fascists and anti-Fascists,
the latter usually communists, were settling old scores. There
were many summary executions. The fate of Mussolini, his
mistress and his Fascist henchmen had not been unique.
Connie thought that probably one side was as bad as another
when it came to brutality. Yet the communists had fought
on the Allied side and, for the time being anyway, had to be
regarded as friends.

There was a sharp knock on the door and Connie froze.
Luisa had a key and no one else ever came to call. She looked
round furtively for somewhere to hide. The knock came again.
She ran upstairs and squeezed herself into the wardrobe in her

bedroom. It was bound to be futile but better than immediately exposing herself to whatever brigand it was – communist or Fascist – who may have got wind of her presence.

For a long time there was silence and, feeling slightly foolish, she was about to leave her hiding place when she heard footsteps on the marble staircase.

She froze again, cowering behind the clothes on the rail in front of her. They would be a poor refuge if a real search was made.

Footsteps sounded in her bedroom. Someone was prowling around. Then they left. She heard them go from one room to another and then, after an eternity, descend the staircase again. There was an exclamation from below; a woman's voice: Luisa's.

"*O Santa Madre!*" Connie heard her exclaim. "*O Signor . . . Signor Allessandro!*" A torrent of words followed in Italian. Connie heard a man's voice and she nearly fainted with shock, clawed frantically at the clothes in front of her, and tumbled out of the wardrobe. Delirious with disbelief she ran across the floor into the corridor and leaned over the banister.

"Alexander!" she shrieked and began tumbling down the stairs. "Oh my God! Alexander!"

Alexander turned, his expression one of shocked surprise and caught Connie just in time as she tripped down the final steps and fell into his arms.

Momentarily they looked into each other's eyes and then they hugged each other for a long time while Luisa dabbed at her eyes.

"I knew you would come back, signor," she said in Italian. "I have looked after the Contessa and kept her safe for you."

"For how long?" Alexander demanded.

Connie drew away from him and replied, "I left Venice a year ago. I have been here ever since."

"A whole year!" Alexander gasped. "What happened to Paolo? Is he here?"

"I will tell you everything," Connie said, still breathless, "but first let's have a drink. I think there are still a few bottles of wine left in your cellar and we can have a celebration."

Luisa made dinner for them: pork loin she had bought in the market, pasta and fresh vegetables and fruit.

The meal was served on the terrace as the moon came up over the lake and there was a bottle of cool crisp Orvieto to drink. Connie had put on the only decent dress she'd managed to bring in the small suitcase she'd escaped with, though God knows why she'd brought it. Maybe in anticipation of an occasion like this. It was a frothy but rather faded blue organdie muslin over a taffeta sheath with a décolleté neckline and a skirt that swept down to her feet on which were a pair of incongruous bright-gold slippers, scarcely ever worn. The whole outfit smelled of must and mothballs, redolent of a bygone era, of better days.

It was ages, perhaps years, since Connie had had her hair done. Once upon a time she had been in the vanguard of fashion, shopping at couture houses under the guidance of Francesca Valenti and in the most exclusive boutiques of Paris, London and Rome. Now she no longer cared what she wore, and it was a long time since she had taken a good look at herself in the mirror. Tonight she had made an effort for Alexander.

Alexander too had made an effort, having changed from the combat uniform in which he'd arrived to a suit, one of many he'd found in his wardrobe. It also smelled of mothballs, had one or two tiny holes where the moths had managed to break through the barrier, and was a little too tight for him now – he hadn't been here since before the war and he'd put on a few inches round the waist.

He supposed that, to an observer, they would look rather a sad, comical pair; but there was no one to see them and neither of them cared. They had both survived a war in which millions had died and that was what mattered.

"On the whole we ate very well during the war," Connie said enjoying her meal in a way she hadn't for years. "There was always meat and plenty of fresh vegetables, better here than in Venice."

"But much more dangerous for you," Alexander looked at her with concern, "with the place running with the Fascists."

"And the Germans. I never went out except sometimes at night to creep round the block. That's why I have such a pallor." Nervously Connie touched her face as if she had suddenly become conscious of the ravages of time. "Luisa looked after me marvellously. I shall have to be sure she is rewarded after I get home and can lay my hands on my money."

"I will reward her too." Alexander gazed around him. "I never expected to find this place so well kept. I thought it would have been occupied and vandalised. I am stationed in Milan and asked for short leave to inspect my property."

"It's a miracle it wasn't. I think it's due to some magic worked by Luisa. Nothing was ever said but I'm sure one of her nephews was with the partisans and they made certain it was left undisturbed. The partisans were just as destructive as the Germans, you know." Connie lowered her voice and then remembered that as they were speaking English Luisa wouldn't understand.

"I do know, and now that the war is over there will be all sorts of trouble as they try and take over the reins of government." Alexander clasped Connie's hand. "I can't tell you how good it is to see you. The family were worried stiff. They will be thrilled to know that you are at least safe. As soon as I get back to my base I'll send them a wire. And Connie, we'll have to get you out of here as soon as we can. I'll see what I can do."

Connie put down her knife and fork, took a sip of wine and folded her hands on the table. Alexander thought how much she had aged; her ash-blonde hair was now partly grey. She was, if he remembered correctly, the same age as his father: fifty-eight. She looked older and so, now, did he. No one was left unaffected by the war.

"Tell me about everyone . . ." Connie sighed deeply.

"I don't know where to begin. My children, of course. Your father. Tell me about everything that has happened to them since the war began and then tell me about yourself, Alexander."

They talked far into the night, sitting on the balcony which had so many memories for Alexander of happier times in the past. But this was a time of happiness too, to know that he and Connie had survived at a period when so many had not.

Connie heard about the death of Jean Parterre with tears in her eyes. About the death of her half-sister Agnes, the disappearance of Bart and Irene, about Minnie and the baby and now the new one she was expecting.

Connie told him about Venice and the death of Paolo, the threat from his son, and her flight across Italy aided by the partisans.

When she finished, she rose and walked restlessly across to the balcony, leaned over it and studied the reflection of the moon on the water.

"Oh, Alexander, I feel so useless. The whole of Europe, nearly the whole world, has been in chaos and it has hardly touched me except that there is not a day when I haven't been afraid, not a day when I didn't wonder about my loved ones, about you all, the children especially. They have reached adulthood without me being there. We will be like strangers. It will be a very difficult adjustment."

"We all have to adjust," Alexander said gently in a vain attempt to comfort her. "I've had five years of fighting and killing. I have shot down at least nineteen planes, killed nineteen pilots, widowed their wives, orphaned their children. It was a case of kill or be killed, but that is a fact. I have strafed people in the streets with bullets. A lot of my comrades have died. I have become very hard. I will find it strange to go back to a desk job, to lead a life of domesticity. I have seen too many horrible things I shan't ever forget." He gazed at Connie for a while trying, in his turn, to imagine the terrible inaction and isolation of her life and the fear that she had lived with daily. He had been surrounded by people. She had had no one. He felt that, given a choice, he rather preferred his five years of danger and intense activity to hers: a seemingly endless period of loneliness and terror, of helplessness, fearing the knock on the door as she had today, of not knowing what was going to happen to her from one day to the next, and largely ignorant about the truth of what was happening in the outside world.

There was still much to tell, but when they went to bed the dawn was breaking . . . a new dawn on a new, and surely less dangerous, but far from happy and settled world?

It was a difficult, even formal reunion. Connie scarcely recognised her children, and at first they were stiff and awkward with her. Children? They were grown up. The last time she had seen them in 1939 Toby had been fourteen, Leonard thirteen and Netta twelve. Now Toby and Leonard were in service uniform. Netta had left school and had wanted to join the WAAF. She'd spent a lot of time talking to Connie and considered it a glamorous career.

Toby and Leonard had met her at Dover and brought her to Pelham's Oak where Carson, Sally and Netta awaited her. They scarcely recognised her as she got rather wearily out of the car and embraced first Netta, a long, long hug, then Carson and Sally. Tall, upright Connie seemed to have shrunk and become a gaunt rather elderly lady, shabbily dressed with greying, lacklustre hair.

Carson had to help her up the steps but her weakness was perhaps due as much to emotion and the strain of her journey as to her homecoming to a place that was no longer home.

"You'll want to rest," Carson said, concern showing on his face as they stood looking at each other in the hall.

"I want a bath," Connie said with a weary smile, running her hands through her lank locks. "I seem to have been travelling for weeks. Alexander arranged transport for me in a succession of military vehicles from Milan to the French coast. I didn't know he was so important, but it was rough going because there were no unoccupied hotels to stay in on the way. It was lovely to get to Dover and see the boys. Of course I hardly recognised them."

"You heard about Agnes?" Carson followed her up the staircase with her small case.

Connie nodded. "And Jean. I heard about Jean. That was terrible. How is Dora?"

"She has coped very well. It's over a year since she heard the news and time does heal. She also had to take care of Louise, and Eliza, although remarkably fit and just as you remember her, is over eighty. Now Dora's anxious to get back to France."

"Will she live in France?"

"I've no idea." Carson threw open one of the bedroom doors.

Connie walked in and looked around.

"Didn't we sleep here when we were first married?"

"You remembered!" Carson smiled.

"Of course I remembered."

"I remember too. But honestly I didn't choose the room, and I'd forgotten until now."

"It *is* a lovely room." Connie wandered over to the window and stood for a few moments looking out. Nothing had changed very much, if at all, since her wedding day twenty-one years before when she had become Lady Woodville but, more importantly, Carson's wife. They had been so much in love. How sad it was that it all had to end.

She turned and saw Carson gazing at her.

"I was thinking about it too," he said. "Our wedding. I'm sorry. They were very happy days. I'm sorry about Paolo."

"Do you mind if we don't talk about it now?" Connie passed a hand across her forehead.

"There's plenty of time." Carson went up to her and kissed her brow. "You rest and relax. You've plenty of time to recover."

"Tell me," Connie called out as he was about to leave the room, "how do you like Minnie?"

"Oh, I like Minnie very much. We all do. We wish they

could get married but," he grimaced, "we'll have to see. We'll know soon, or we should do, if Irene is alive or dead."

Surrounded by the family, especially her children, getting to know them again, Connie gradually felt a sense of peace returning. She had been so isolated for so long, speaking Italian all the time that she almost thought in Italian. Her family teased her that she had a foreign accent. She thought she probably had.

She went up to London, stayed a few days, had her hair restyled and coloured and bought clothes. Lally had hoarded her coupons and gave her some. She felt like a new woman, walking on air.

She met Minnie, whom she took to at once. She saw Dora, Eliza, Sophie and Hubert and they shed lots of tears together. Gradually she was able to come to terms with the past, to feel her old self again. She lost that gaunt, haunted look – the result of years of fear – and recovered her old poise and élan.

Netta had never been to Agnes's house. To her she had been a strange, remote old lady who she never thought of as 'grandmama'.

"Of course she was not my real grandmother," Netta said as she and her mother wandered from one room to the other.

"She was your grandfather's second wife and was your step-grandmother."

"Did you like her, Mum?"

"Not much, if I'm honest," Connie said thoughtfully. "She could be poisonous, but she had led an interesting life and an unfortunate one. In many ways she was the victim of her own greed, but she was my half-sister and I felt an obligation to her, which was why when she fell on hard times I let her have this house. Now it has reverted to me and I can do what I like with it."

"And you lived in this house when you were small?"

"Yes." Feeling deeply nostalgic Connie looked around. It was very different from when, as a rather plain, lonely child with few friends of her own age, but a beautiful singing voice she had lived under the watchful, doting eye of Miss Fairchild. In those days she had always felt she would be a spinster like her guardian and never dreamt that, eventually, she would be married twice and have three beautiful children of her own, as well as a fortune.

Aware of Netta's sympathetic, but watchful, eye on her Connie interrupted her reverie.

"The house originally belonged to my guardian, Miss Fairchild. She adopted me when my father died. She was a very sweet person, very good to me. Very kind. She died in Venice during the first war and is buried there."

"Are we going to go back to Venice?"

Netta flopped on the sofa and Connie sat next to her, reached for her daughter's hand.

"I notice you say 'we'. Would you like to?"

"But you say the palazzo is no longer ours?"

"That will take some time to sort out. The Valentis weren't sure that Giacomo had a right to it and if he is in any way tainted with Fascism it may be that it could be confiscated and we could get it from him."

"Would you like to live there again?"

Connie stared up at the ceiling. "I'm not sure I would. My last years in Italy were not happy ones. If I did go back to Venice I think I might buy another place. But somehow I have gone off Venice, and the rest of Europe is in tatters. I think I might stay here, for a while at least."

"In this house?" Netta looked surprised.

"Why not? It's a nice house."

"It's very small." Netta grimaced and Connie smiled at her fondly. Netta was a beauty. Very like her father, she was tall with thick ash-blonde hair scraped back into a pony tail. She had blue eyes which could twinkle with merriment, though in repose her expression was grave. She had missed her mother and had worried about her. Since Connie's return she hardly ever left her side. Now her mother realised how little she knew about her beloved child.

"What do you want to do, Netta?" Connie still had hold of her hand. "I mean do you want to get a job or what?"

"I wanted to go into the WAAF, but it's too late now. I feel I'd like to do something useful, help people recovering from the war. Do you know what I mean? There must be lots of damaged people and I'd like to help them. Did you see those awful pictures of the concentration camps? I couldn't get them out of my mind."

"You are very young, darling, for that sort of thing. It will be very harrowing. Tell me," she gave a tactful cough, "how have you got on with Sally?"

"Sally is very sweet. Very nice. She went out of her way to be good to us." Netta nodded approvingly. "I like her. Only . . ." she paused.

"Yes?"

"Well I don't know that I should tell you this; but I don't think she and Dad get on too well. I don't think they're very happy."

"I'm sorry." Connie looked thoughtful. "I'm genuinely sorry about that."

"Of course, they led very busy, different lives during the war. Dad was commander of the local Home Guard and then he did an awful lot to develop the farming side of Pelham's Oak and support the war effort. Sally was into the WVS, Mrs Churchill's aid to Russia, that sort of thing."

"You would have thought that would have given them something in common."

"I've never heard them row. There's just a lack of togetherness. Besides, they sleep in different rooms."

"How long has this being going on?"

"I noticed it last summer when I got back from school. There is a distance between them, a sort of formality that you never had with Paolo. Mum . . ." Netta looked keenly at her mother, "why did you and Dad split up? I think you're much more his type than Sally. Was it Paolo?"

159

"Oh no! That's not why we split up." Connie hesitated for a moment and then continued. "Your father had an old girlfriend whom he brought here when she was ill. He expected me to look after her. I thought that was a bit much. I suppose I was jealous. I felt he thought more of her than me and I think he did, as a matter of fact." She pursed her mouth stubbornly.

"That was Alexander's mother?"

"Oh, well then, if you know that, you know it all."

"I thought it was something to do with her, but Dad would never talk about it. No one would."

"I went back to Venice and Paolo was there. He had always wanted to marry me, so we got married. Your father had met Sally and I thought it would all work out very well."

"I think Dad would much prefer you. He was very excited about the thought of you coming back."

"Oh dear!" Connie leaned back against the sofa and smiled. "It's a bit like history repeating itself. In that case I had better not stay too long at Pelham's Oak. I would hate to do to Sally what Nelly did to me. Do you know," she rose and began to pace around the room, "I do like this house; I will have it done up, refurnish it. I don't want to outstay my welcome at Pelham's Oak."

"Mum!" Netta burst out, her eyes suddenly filling with tears. "It *is* good to have you back. You don't know how much I've missed you."

"Me too, darling. But I'm so glad you weren't trapped in Italy as I was. I can't think what might have happened to us all then."

Connie flung her arms round her daughter's neck and pressed her close, very close – that vibrant, pulsating young body that at times she thought she might never see or touch again. It had been terrible having the children grow up so far away from her, but at least they'd been safe. They were alive, and how many parents in many parts of war-torn Europe – in the debris of Berlin, the gutters of Warsaw or the dreadful desolation of the concentration camps – could say that?

Twelve

October 1945

The Second World War had ended in August after two atomic bombs were dropped on Japan signalling the end of one era and the beginning of another: the Atomic age. In this most brutal and widespread of wars it was later to be estimated that fifty million people had died, though the true total damage was probably incalculable if one included shattered minds and bodies and broken lives.

Alexander was still a serving member of the Royal Air Force but he was anxious to obtain his demobilisation papers and return to civilian life. Accordingly he had permission to spend days in his office which, happily, had survived the blitz, and try and restore the remnants of his business.

In 1939, Alexander had been about to take over from Pieter Heering as chairman, and since then Pieter, though in his seventies, had managed to keep the company going but only just. It was not the mighty business empire it had been, because to expand or diversify in the war – other than by providing ships requisitioned by the Merchant Navy – had been impossible, and all trade with the Far East had come to a virtual standstill. Their ships had formed a valuable part of the Merchant Navy during the war, carrying food from America to England or Russia in convoy, and several had been sunk with great loss of life.

The warehouses in Thames Street, where all the imports from the East had been stored were now empty, cavernous places, except for rats, but still with the lingering smells of spice and essential oils which perfumed the narrow streets around.

Minnie had given birth to their second son just as peace had been declared. In honour of the peace he was called Christian. Their first son had been named Francis after Minnie's father, who was always known as Frank. She was still living with Lally in the country and Alexander's dearest wish was to set up home with her and their children and, if possible, marry her.

He had made many enquiries, and caused them to be made, in the ruins of Berlin and beyond about Irene, but no news had been forthcoming. As the true horrors of the concentration camps emerged, and were still emerging, his conviction grew that she had perished in the gas chambers. If only one could know for sure one could then make respectful arrangements for honouring her memory.

During the war Alexander had kept in touch with Irene's parents Reuben and Alma Schwartz, who had remained at their home in Golder's Green hoping for news of their daughter. To them it was a terrible irony that Irene had so foolishly returned to Berlin in an attempt to rescue a friend.

Reuben had died the previous year, probably of grief brought on by the strain of war, and Alexander had kept an eye on Alma who scarcely ever left her flat, the victim of nervous prostration.

It might well be years before anyone knew what had happened to Irene, if ever, and one day he would apply to the authorities to assume her death; but that day, inevitably, was far off.

Alexander, in his shirt sleeves, had just finished dictating letters to his secretary. He glanced at his watch and reached for his jacket. There was a dinner of old comrades at the RAF Club and he wanted to go home, have a bath and change. He then had a free weekend which he would spend in the country with Minnie and the children before returning on Monday to his base, hopefully to begin the final formalities for his demobilisation. He had enjoyed service life, his adventurous war, but he knew he would not miss it.

The telephone on his desk rang and he answered it.

"There's someone on the line for you, Mr Alexander," his secretary said. "The sound is very faint. I think it's from abroad."

Alexander's heart somersaulted. He recalled the exact circumstances when he had last heard from Irene in 1939. But this time it was a man's voice, speaking not too indistinctly after all, with an American accent.

"Mr Martyn?"

"Yes, Alexander Martyn speaking."

"Mr Martyn, you don't know me but I'm a doctor at an American hospital outside Berlin."

"Yes?" Alexander's heart began to beat faster.

"I have a lady here who says she is your wife. Irene? Is that right?"

"That is correct. You mean my wife . . . Irene is alive and well? I haven't heard from her since 1939."

"She has a remarkable story, Mr Martyn, and she is alive but she is not at all well. She hovered near death for several weeks, and for months after that she was unable to recall who she was, but she is recovering and her memory has begun to return in the last few days, which is why we have only just been able to find out anything about her. I know she would like to see you. I'm sure you would like to see her."

"Could you give me the details?" Alexander said picking up a pen and beginning to write on a piece of paper. As he did so his hand was shaking.

The American hospital was in a convent still run by an order of enclosed German nuns. By some miracle it had escaped the bombing. It was a large Gothic building, with its own chapel, set in woodland.

Inside, the nuns, who had made all the facilities of the convent available to the authorities, had managed to maintain a calm atmosphere of tranquillity and efficiency. Where they could they abandoned their vow of silence and assisted with the nursing.

"Mrs Martyn was found in a distressed state in a cellar in one of the bombed-out buildings right in the centre of Berlin Templehof shortly after the liberation. Apparently she and a handful of Jews had spent most of the war living like this, moving from place to place . . . like rats, to use her own words, in a cellar."

"And were the others with her?"

"Only one." The medical superintendent lowered his eyes. "She was dead. I'm afraid you will be distressed by your wife's condition, but she is much better than when she came in."

"Much better." The sister who had accompanied Alexander nodded encouragingly. "I didn't think she would last the night. She had no identification you see so we could not contact you."

"May I see her?" Alexander, having recovered from his shock, stood up. "Will she recognise me?"

"Oh, I think she will." The nursing sister smiled. "It is whether or not *you* will recognise *her*."

The white-haired old lady lying in a corner bed of the ward was certainly not Irene. Alexander felt again that familiar sense of despair that meant he was still as far from the truth as he had even been. There had been a mistake. He stood looking down at her and shook his head.

"She is not my wife," he said turning to the nun. "There is some mistake."

"Irene Martyn," the nurse said pointing to a tag on the patient's wrist, "aged thirty-three. Is that right?" The sister then consulted a file she was carrying in her hand. "She is now perfectly lucid when she is awake. She says she was born in Berlin in 1912, her parents are Alma and Reuben Schwartz. She married Alexander Martyn in London in July 1939."

"Then it is Irene." Alexander bent more closely to scrutinise the face of the woman on the bed whereupon her eyelids fluttered and those dark, luminous, clearly recognisable eyes stared out at him appearing at first to have difficulty focusing.

"Irene," he whispered sitting on the side of her bed and taking her hand.

"Alexander?" She looked at him wonderingly. "Is it you?"

"It's me all right." He smiled, but he could not bring himself to bend and kiss her. Her cheeks were so sunken that it was almost possible to imagine that one was staring at a cadaver who had somehow been brought to life, if life it could be called. He could see how thin and emaciated her body was through the bedclothes that covered her.

"You're in uniform." She put out a skeletal hand and touched his arm. "The air force?"

He nodded.

"Perhaps you bombed Berlin?"

"No." His throat was so constricted that he found it hard to speak. "I never bombed Berlin. I was in fighters."

"That's good." She turned her head away. "Then you didn't bomb me."

"Oh, Irene!" Alexander lowered his head and the tears that he had fought so hard to control welled up behind his eyes. "You have no idea what torture we have been through not knowing how you were or where."

"I think that is enough now Group Captain Martyn," the nurse said gently, taking his elbow. "We shall have to go little by little, day by day. It is all very strange for her."

And little by little, day by day it was. Because it was all very strange for Alexander too.

January 1946

Connie threw her napkin down on the table and, leaning back in her chair, gazed at the others.

"Well I'm delighted to say the house is now ready for occupation. It is looking very nice isn't it Netta?"

Netta agreed. "Very nice, Mum. Nice but small."

"Small if you are used to living at Pelham's Oak or in an Italian palazzo; but don't forget I lived in that house as a child. I am used to it and I love it."

Carson reached over for the cheese, a frown on his face. David moved over to pour him more wine.

"Is this claret pre-war, David?"

"Pre which war, sir?" David asked with a superior smile.

"Of course I meant the First World War. I get my wars mixed up."

"1902, Sir Carson. A very rare vintage."

"It is very good." Carson raised the glass to his lips. "Don't you agree, Dora?"

Dora nodded. "Excellent. You should treasure your fine wines, Carson. Good wines will be hard to come by until the French wine industry recovers."

They were at Sunday lunch at Pelham's Oak, the sort of family occasion Carson so enjoyed. Dora and Eliza had come over. Toby and Leonard had not yet been demobilised. Carson longed for normality to return so that he could resume the life that suited him of country squire and farmer, father of the family.

After the discussion about the wine he looked across at Connie.

"There is no need for you to live at Agnes's house at all. Aren't you happy here?"

"Of course I'm happy, Carson, but this is not my home. I feel that, for various reasons, I can't yet go back to Italy. I shall be moving out next week."

"Not Netta too, I hope?" Carson looked anxiously at his daughter.

"I'm going to London, Daddy, to try and find a job.

"Now why do you need a job?"

"Daddy, I can't stay here for ever, either."

"Carson wants all his family about him." Eliza smiled

fondly at her nephew. "I think I know why. The war has made us all restless, rootless." She put her hand on the arm of Dora sitting next to her. "Dora will soon be going back to France for good. I shall feel lost too."

Dora had been back and forth since France had been liberated, but was too restless without Jean to stay long.

"You have to accept that things change, Carson," Sally said. "People have their own lives to lead. They can't all be dictated to by you."

"I am *not* dictating *anything* to *anyone*." Carson looked at her angrily. "What a stupid thing to say."

Connie felt embarrassed. She had been here long enough to know that, as Netta had said, all was not well between Carson and his wife, and she was frequently distressed when they had their tiffs in public, as they increasingly did. It was an uncomfortable atmosphere in which to live and she was, in fact, quite anxious to be gone and had hurried on the decorators. In addition she had spent a lot of time in London buying new carpets, wallpaper and furniture and had scoured the countryside for antiques.

Rose Cottage was not exactly a cottage but a pretty little house and it would suit her very well for the time being.

Carson's remark had been followed by an awkward silence. Sally had bitten her lip and had then got on with her cheese and biscuits.

"Has anyone been to see Irene lately?" Eliza broke the silence at last. "She's looking very much better."

"I can't get over that white hair," Carson said. "It makes her look about seventy."

"But she has a young face, the colour is returning to her cheeks and she's putting on weight at last. You can see some of her old attraction returning."

"But what a situation!" Carson said. "It's intolerable for Alexander."

"And not very nice for Minnie, though she is being a brick."

Eliza, a frequent visitor, continued to look troubled. The

return of Irene, wholly unexpected had, it must be confessed, been a shock to the family. They all loved Minnie who had been so happily ensconced in the cottage with her two babies, awaiting Alexander's demob. But always that shadow had hung over them.

And then Alexander had returned from Germany in a private ambulance with his wife who had been installed in Forest House together with a team of nurses to look after her.

Irene had been suffering from all kinds of symptoms, the root cause of which was severe malnutrition. She had to be very gradually reintroduced to food and her health carefully monitored.

"Does Irene realise who Minnie is?" Sally, who had yet to visit the invalid, asked.

"She does now," Eliza replied. "Alexander had to tell her."

"How did she react?"

"She didn't seem very surprised. She's still a very sick woman."

Dora shook her head. "It is a very, very awkward situation. I haven't a clue how they'll resolve it."

"Anyone for coffee?" Sally drew back her chair. "Shall we have it in the drawing room?"

Netta wound up the gramophone and Sally poured coffee. Carson filled his pipe and stood with his back to the fire.

"I don't know why you want to go to London?" he grumbled to Netta. "There's plenty for you to do here."

"Like what, Daddy?"

"Riding. You enjoy that. You can help in the stables – we're short-staffed."

"I would really prefer to help with the refugees in Germany," Netta replied stubbornly.

"You'd have to have some training for that." Dora took her coffee to a chair by the fire. "They wouldn't take a young girl like you without training."

"What sort of training?"

"Nursing? Have you thought of that?"

"But that will take *ages*. I want to do it *now*."

"Maybe some sort of secretarial work?" Eliza suggested. "I agree with Dora. You would be more of a hindrance than a help without some kind of training."

"I wish I'd been old enough to go into the WAAF while the war was still on," Netta said sulkily. "They'd have allowed me to go then."

Dora jumped up and looked out of the window.

"It's stopped raining. I'm going for a ride. Carson?"

"I have to do some paperwork. We still have to think of our quotas."

"Connie?"

But Connie had never been keen on riding and shook her head.

"I'll come with you." Sally rose and stretched. "I could do with the exercise."

"I shall go and have a snooze," Eliza said. "Netta, are you going to go riding?"

"I'm going to look out my things for London." Netta looked defiantly at her father. "Do you think Alexander will let me stay at Montagu Square?"

"I'm sure he will," Carson said sighing deeply, "but I can't think why you want to go anywhere. You could be perfectly happy here."

"Happiness isn't really the point is it?" Dora remarked to Sally as, having changed into riding clothes, they made their way over to the stables. "I mean Netta is a modern young woman and Carson is still living in the past. Carson had his family all during the war which is more than Connie had."

Sally said nothing but tapped her crop against her thigh as they stood by the stables deciding which horses they would ride.

Sally was something of an enigma to Dora. She fascinated her too. Maybe it was because she was so quiet, almost secretive. One never could be sure what was going on in her mind. She was outwardly so kind, polite and cheerful, but her manner lacked sincerity and, with it, warmth. Dora always imagined that for some reason Sally still felt herself to be a stranger.

"I think I'll take Pegasus," Sally said opening the stable door of a fine roan. "He hasn't been out for a while."

"And I'll take Caesar." Dora undid the door of a horse who was a direct descendant of her mother's horse, Lady, on which her mother had eloped so many years before with Dora's father.

After they had saddled the horses and taken them over to the paddock Dora said, "It is strange to think that Caesar and his family were bred here from Lady, my mother's horse when she was eighteen."

"You've got a very strong sense of family," Sally said, gracefully mounting Pegasus, "even among the horses."

"Do I detect a note of bitterness?" Dora mounted Caesar and they set out at a trot across the paddock towards the fields. "Or is it sarcasm? After all you're family too."

"But not a Woodville."

"I would have thought you were, very much so, by marriage at least, Lady Woodville."

Again Sally didn't reply but dug her heels into the flank of the horse and set off at a brisk canter across the fields towards the cottage where Ryder had lived before he and Eliza eloped. It was a pretty, white-washed, thatched cottage set in a valley about a mile away from the big house. It had quite a history. Apart from the romance of Ryder and Eliza, in more recent times Carson had brought Alexander's mother, Nelly, there and that was where she had died.

Dora followed more slowly. Like the rest of the family she was aware of the tension between Carson and Sally. However much they tried to disguise it there were always those little eruptions in public, like the outburst at luncheon today. It worried them that when Connie returned Carson had paid her so much attention. But then that was so like Carson, always the do-gooder, always helping those in trouble, as Connie had been, as Nelly had before her. Whatever Carson's motivation, Dora was quite sure it was not solely to do with past loves. He had given Jean a home when he had been uprooted by the First World War, and his half-sister Elizabeth, together with her husband and three children, had virtually taken over Pelham's Oak when he found them living in poverty.

He was an intrinsically good man and now it seemed as though his mantle had fallen on Alexander with perhaps equally unfortunate, or potentially unfortunate, results. Neither of them could say 'no'. But then Alexander was in a more invidious situation than Carson had ever been, as Irene was his lawful wife and was desperately in need of help in a way that Connie, with her wealth, had not.

While Dora was thinking these rather sombre thoughts Sally, ahead of her, had alighted from Pegasus and was standing looking up at the cottage, hands on her hips, as Dora joined her.

"This could do with a fresh coat of paint," she said turning to Dora. "In fact I think the whole place needs doing up." She walked along the garden path and pushed the front door which opened quite easily.

"Does no one live here now?" Dora asked.

"No, but it shouldn't be left unlocked. Maybe it's broken." Dora followed Sally inside.

It was many years since she'd visited the scene of her parents' romance in 1880. It was strange to think that two world wars had intervened since then. It was equally strange to think of her venerable mother, now in her mid-eighties, as that wayward, headstrong girl who had caused the aristocratic Woodvilles such anguish by eloping with a handsome thatcher.

The inside of the cottage was cheerful despite the drabness of the day, though a pale wintry sun had finally emerged to inveigle them out of doors.

The furniture was charmingly rustic with chintz-covered chairs and a well-polished oak table with a brass urn in the middle. The inglenook fireplace had no glow in it, but logs were neatly piled up on one side.

"The whole place could do with a lick of paint," Sally said. "I must tell Carson. As to your enquiry," she gazed across at Dora, "no one lives here since Massie went to look after Minnie's babies. I think she has found a more or less permanent home with them."

"Will you let it?"

"I thought I might live here myself." Sally sat down on one of the chairs, her hands thrust deep in the pockets of her jodphurs. She looked across at Dora who had perched on the arm of the chair opposite her. "Why not?"

"I would have thought . . . it would upset Carson."

"Carson has Connie."

"Oh, that's very silly, Sally."

"No it isn't." Sally's mouth set in a stubborn line. "You can see for yourself how he looks at her all the time. How aware he is of her. He doesn't want her to go and live in Agnes's house."

"But she does."

"Does she? I wonder." Sally looked thoughtfully at the ceiling.

"You can't possibly be jealous of Connie! I mean . . . that was over years ago."

Sally got up and went and stood in front of the fireplace staring for a few seconds into the empty grate. Then she turned and gazed at Dora.

"I don't think it was ever over. I think that Carson regretted losing Connie and has remained in love with her. He married me on the rebound and the flame didn't burn for long.

"Since she's came back he's hardly ever left her side. He's like a ridiculous puppy with a new owner. He put her in the bedroom where they slept after they were first married. He said he had forgotten it was that the room, but I don't think he did." Sally paused, then continued in a quiet voice, "We haven't slept together for years. Look . . . they had three children together. He and I had none. It was my fault. My own

172

inadequacy. It must have been. He had already produced four children. He and Connie have much more in common than he and I ever had.

"I like his kids and I think they like me. I'm a good stepmother to them. But we aren't *close*. Carson clucks after them like an old hen; he is continually anxious about them. I can never feel that way. Let him and Connie share their concern together. I've done my bit."

Dora stayed silent reflecting that Sally was right. She remembered how the birth of Louise, after years of sterile marriage, had made her and Jean so much closer. It was true that children formed an unbreakable bond, whether it was for good or ill. What would Alexander do about Irene, now he and Minnie were the parents of two babies?

"Look," she said getting up and walking slowly across to Sally, "I shall be going back to France again soon. I have to. We have some new vines to plant, lots of repairs to do or else the business will collapse."

"And you want to keep it going?"

"Of course." Dora looked surprised. "That's what Jean would have wanted. I want it too, in his memory."

"You must have loved him a lot," Sally said wistfully putting her arm round Dora's waist as if to comfort her. The gesture surprised and touched Dora.

"I did and I do. Come and stay with me for a while. Much better than moving in here because that would cause a real rift. I can say that I need some help and you offered. It won't seem at all strange. Then you can decide what you want to do."

"I already know what I want to do," Sally said slowly. "I want to divorce Carson. He is no longer in love with me or I with him. We grate on each other, have done for ages. It's sad but it is a fact. We'd both be happier apart. He loves Connie and should never have divorced her." She smiled sadly up at Dora. "What you say makes a lot of sense. It *would* cause a terrible rift and embarrass Carson in front of the staff and his family. I don't want to do that. If you really need me, want me, I think I'd like to go."

"I'm so glad," Dora said with a sigh and putting her arm round Sally, hugged her.

Momentarily she felt closer to her than she had to anyone, except Louise, since Jean had died.

Thirteen

February 1946

E ngland took a long time to recover from the war. Churchill, the architect of victory, had been unceremoniously thrown out by the electorate and a Labour Government had been returned in 1945. A Welfare State was in the process of being established with the intention of looking after the populace from the cradle to the grave, but no one could doubt that the task of post-war reconstruction at home was a huge one. Ironically, the faltering business that had once been run by Bart Sadler was now riding on a crest. Rebuilding bombed-out houses and manufacturing prefabricated homes for people who had lost theirs in the war, or for soldiers returning home, was a growth industry.

Sam was not interested in the business. He felt too restless. Having served in the army throughout the reconquest of Europe he had been one of the first to apply for demobilisation. He had had enough of war; in the process, in his disillusionment and the end of any ideals about the nobility of man, he had lost himself. He felt he'd almost lost the will to live and that it was a pity so many men with families had died, whereas, he, with no one who particularly loved him, had been spared.

Of course he had his family. His mother, Sophie Turner, was clearly pleased to see him back. His half-sisters, Ruth and Deborah, even his half-bother, Timothy, greeted him with what seemed genuine pleasure and relief. But there was no father, no Bart and, at times Sam, who had known him so briefly, ached to see him again. He could not imagine life in Wenham without him. Surely what had started so well couldn't just finish? The pride and joy his father had in him had given new meaning to a life of adolescent delinquency and subsequent discontent.

For the first time he had felt that here was someone who cared for him, loved him and understood him in a way his mother or stepfather had never even tried. In the light of what he subsequently found out – that Bart and his mother had been lovers – he knew that, in her heart of hearts, and being overtly religious, she felt he was a child of sin and was ashamed of him. Most certainly she wished he had never been born, and thus she had never given him the unconditional love she gave to her other children. Although Hubert Turner had done his best, that pious churchman was as different from Bart as chalk was to cheese. Deborah had understood him and, he thought, loved him in her funny selfish way. One always had the impression that the only person Deborah really cared for was herself. She had not been a good wife to Bart.

Deborah and Abel had been quite prepared to welcome Sam back into the business. They had gone out of their way to show him plans and projected figures with some excitement. But he wasn't interested.

He felt lost, strange, out of place. His only desire was to find his father, and now that Irene had so unexpectedly returned from the dead, might there not be a possibility that in some bombed-out cellar or refugee camp he might find Bart, perhaps suffering from loss of memory, with no idea of his past or who he was?

Sam had been very anxious to talk to Irene who, after all, might have been the last one to see Bart; but he was kept away from her. She was to have no visitors other than her husband, mother-in-law and close relations, who would not ask her awkward questions or remind her of the past.

When he had brought her home Alexander had thought

he would soon be burying her beside his mother in Wenham churchyard, such was her frailty. Her memory lapsed again and she appeared to have no idea who Lally was.

For a time she once again hovered between life and death, but now she was definitely on the mend, able to walk about her room and go downstairs if she felt like it, but still very delicate.

"Please don't ask her too many questions," Alexander said to Sam as he took him up to Irene's room, "or stay too long. You don't mind if I stay with you?"

"Of course not," Sam said rather brusquely. "After all, she is your wife."

"Don't misunderstand me, Sam. Irene has been very, very ill. It is doubtful if she will ever be completely well again."

Irene was sitting in a chair by the window as Sam and Alexander entered the room. She did not turn her head and Sam thought – rather as Alexander had when he first saw her in hospital – that he was looking at the wrong person: that shock of snowy-white hair was not what he had expected.

However, when she turned he saw that it was Irene, who he didn't know very well and had only met a few times at family gatherings at Forest House or Pelham's Oak. But she'd been striking, impressive with her dark vivacious good looks, smart appearance and plenty of make-up. Someone you didn't forget. Now he felt he was looking at a ghost.

But the eyes still sparkled and she wore a little make-up. He saw there was a stick by her chair and her knees were covered with a rug.

"Forgive me if I don't get up," she said extending a hand towards him. "Sam, it is very good to see you again."

"I didn't think you'd remember me," he said, taking her hand.

"It was a long time ago." She still had a silvery, mellifluous voice. Her skin was youthful. Some people did go prematurely grey and it suited them. He rather thought that, regretful though the circumstances were, it suited Irene.

"Would you like coffee, dear?" Alexander bent solicitously over her. "Would you like me to leave you alone with Sam for a while?"

"No," she put up a restraining hand, "do stay. You might help me to remember. I'm sure we'd both like coffee, wouldn't we, Sam?"

"Please." Sam gingerly took the chair Alexander had placed for him by Irene's side.

"He fusses after me such a lot." Irene laughed as Alexander left the room. "I am spoilt rotten."

"I hear you had a terrible time in the war," Sam said anxious not to upset her.

"It was a terrible time to be trapped in a place like Berlin surrounded by enemies: the enemy within and the enemy without. We were hunted by the Nazis, Berlin was bombed to smithereens by the Allies, and then the Russians arrived." A cloud seemed to pass across her face. "However . . . it is all over. I survived. Many didn't. And I hear you were badly wounded at Dunkirk?"

"I survived too." Sam no longer liked to discuss his part in the war. "And I fought right through from D-Day to VE day. I am just glad it's all over, Irene." Sam moved his chair closer to hers as Alexander entered carrying a tray with three cups of coffee. Giving Sam and Irene theirs, he pulled up a chair and sat between them.

"Did you discuss anything?" he asked anxiously.

"Only the war, which we both want to forget."

"Exactly!" Alexander seemed to agree.

"But there is one thing I don't want to forget." Sam moved uneasily in his chair. "I don't want to forget Bart."

"Of course you don't." Irene spoke from the heart. "I don't want to forget him either."

"So you did see him?" Sam's eyes lit up.

"Yes I did. I think I might have unwittingly been the cause of his arrest."

"He was actually arrested?" Sam's heart began to thump painfully and he moved even nearer to Irene, whose voice had sunk almost to a whisper, anxious not to miss a thing.

"He was taken away by the Gestapo. I don't know what happened to him after that."

"He was actually *arrested* by the Gestapo?" Sam's voice also sank to a whisper.

"I was in his apartment when they came. It was like this."

She then told him about the events of that far-off evening in Berlin when a message had brought her to Bart and the Gestapo had soon followed.

"As I looked out of the window," she concluded, "I saw a man watching the car with Bart and the Gestapo inside drive off. I believe that man might have been someone who Bart had mentioned to me as a colleague or business associate of his who might be able to get us out of the country. He said it was he who got Father out of the concentration camp. His name, if I recall it correctly, was Anton Lippe."

Sam tapped his forehead.

"You've heard of him?" Irene looked puzzled.

"The name rings a bell." Sam shook his head. "I can't think how. Maybe it will come to me."

Irene took Sam's hand, her expression one of sadness.

"I am so sorry Sam, but I don't think Bart can be alive. The Gestapo gave short shrift to people who helped the Jews. Believe me, if I have been the cause of his death I can't tell you how sorry I am. The burden will remain with me, along with many others, for the rest of my life."

And silently Irene began to weep.

"I think you'd better go," Alexander whispered to him. "She tires so easily."

Sam left Alexander to see to Irene and went downstairs. For a moment he stood in the huge hall and compared it with Upper Park, the mansion where he now lived alone. It was much too big for him. Without Bart, he found it too gloomy and solitary. He was shaken by the news about Bart and as he let himself out and crossed the lawn towards his car he was wracking his brain trying to remember where he'd heard the name Anton Lippe before, because he certainly had.

In front of him a woman was walking with a couple of dogs bounding along ahead of her. He had no idea who she was but as he approached his car she slowed down and looked behind her. She was a tall, attractive brunette wearing a loose jacket over a pullover and slacks and she smiled at him.

"Hello," she said.

"Hello." Sam stopped and held out his hand. "I'm Sam Turner."

"I'm Minnie Fisher."

"Oh!" Sam looked at her again.

"I see you know who I am."

"You're Alexander's . . ." he paused.

"Quite." The smile faded and her tone became brittle. "No one quite knows what to call me."

"I'm sorry if I offended you. I'm Sophie's son. Bart Sadler was my father."

Minnie nodded as if she knew all about him. "I suppose you've been to see Irene. Alexander told me all about Bart, although I never met him."

"I knew him for such a brief time," Sam said sadly. "I loved him so much . . ."

"Was Irene any help?" Minnie's tone was warm, sympathetic. "Look, my cottage is just over there. Why don't you come and have a coffee and tell me all about it?"

"I feel embarrassed," Sam said.

"Don't be. I'd like you to. I think it would help." Minnie called to the dogs who followed them obediently as she and Sam walked round to the cottage and went inside.

She saw Sam into the sitting room then went and got coffee. Sam was gazing out of the window when she reappeared.

"It's a nice place," he said.

"You were never here before?" Minnie carefully put down the tray and poured the coffee.

"I've been at Forest House with my mother and stepfather,

180

but my father was never very friendly with the Woodville family. I suppose you know all about that."

"A bit." Minnie passed him his cup with a smile. He thought she was extraordinarily attractive.

"Tell me what Irene said," she suggested. "It clearly upset you."

"It seems that my father was arrested by the Gestapo. Irene saw it. We never knew what happened to him and now we do. It's a link. It is very doubtful – in fact almost impossible – to believe that he survived the war."

"I'm so sorry." Minnie's beautiful eyes brimmed with sympathy and she passed him the cigarette box. Sam took a cigarette, lit hers and then his own. "The war has affected so many people." She sounded sad too. "I lost my husband."

"Yes I know. I'm sorry."

Minnie gazed at the tip of her cigarette. "I suppose you know all about Irene?"

"Yes." Sam hesitated.

"You can talk about it. I don't mind. In fact . . ." she looked round the room, "I'm thinking of moving. I don't know if you know of anywhere that might be suitable. A house . . . not too small. This is rather cramped. It was supposed to be temporary, now it seems it could last for ever."

Sam frowned. "I don't really understand. I thought you and Alexander—"

"Were going to get married? Is that what you mean? That was before we found Irene was alive. The situation is now not what it was. Irene is a very sick woman and Alexander can't possibly leave her. I quite realise that. He is in an awful situation and I'd be a monster if I didn't understand."

"But she does know about you?"

"Oh yes, but we haven't met. She doesn't go out and I no longer visit the house. It has changed everything. It had to. I can't go on living here as Alexander's mistress. It wouldn't be right and, besides, I don't want to. It's not a situation I like, or want, to continue.

"You see Alexander is too fine a person to want that either. He is a soul in torment, poor lamb. The very best thing is for me to move away."

"I have a very large house," Sam said suddenly. "I am going to go abroad to try to find my father. It might take months, even years. The house will be empty except for the servants. You are more than welcome to move in there with your children, and the nursemaid of course. You can stay there for as long as you like."

"Oh, I couldn't."

"But why not?" Sam took another cigarette from the box. "The house was built for a family, not just one man. I shall put it on the market if I return without Father and by then your own situation might have resolved itself. I assure you you will not be compromised in the least because I shan't be there."

He smiled disarmingly. "No one could possibly call it improper. It will give you time to sort yourself out and decide what to do, and you will be doing me a favour making use of the house. It has been sadly neglected during the war with only a skeleton staff." Sam appeared like a man transformed by his suggestion and looked eagerly down at her. "Say 'yes'?"

"I'll think about it," Minnie said slowly, thoughtfully. "I will think about it very carefully indeed."

To everyone's astonishment Abel had left his wife and now lived openly with Deborah in her home on the far side of Wenham. The family was shocked, the neighbourhood scandalised. In fact if it had not happened during the war no one would have talked about anything else for weeks.

Only Ruth seemed to have taken it relatively calmly. Her husband had left her and she had resolutely got on with her good works. She had long been suspicious of his reasons and excuses for spending so much time away from home, and she entertained no illusions about her sister. Ruth and Abel had no children, and had gradually grown apart. She had a comfortable home, a good income and plenty of friends. Besides, times were changing radically. Morals were not what they were; illicit liaisons were being formed all over the place. People now tolerated things that would have shocked them to the core before the war.

Deborah listened to Sam's account of his visit to Irene and noticed his air of suppressed excitement, so much so that at first she thought the news about Bart must be good.

Sam had come into the office that morning with the élan, the spring in his step of a man rejuvenated and, despite the depressing news he had to give them about Bart, Irene had given him hope.

"You remember years ago we found the name of someone in Switzerland Bart use to do business with, Anton Lippe?"

Deborah shook her head.

"It was about forty-two or three. I was still in hospital and you told me about it."

"Oh, I think I do remember." Deborah's tone was preoccupied. She was busy looking at plans for a new housing development in the Purbecks on the table before her. Nowadays she was the complete businesswoman and seldom thought of anything else, let alone an event that had happened four or five years before. Anyway she was quite sure Bart was dead and that was that.

"Do you think you could find that reference anywhere Deborah?"

"Is it *really* necessary?"

"Yes, it is," Sam said firmly. "I know you don't care about Bart any more, but I do."

"Of *course* I care about Bart." Deborah turned to him indignantly. "I mean I care about what happens to him, but," she gestured helplessly, "I am quite sure that, after all this time, he must be dead. Bart would always have found a way of getting out if he'd been able to. You know Bart."

Sam turned away, suddenly depressed again. Yes, he knew Bart who had never let anybody deflect him from his aim; who, more than most people, had an almost miraculous way of overcoming all odds. In his heart of hearts he knew Deborah was right, must be right.

"There is a file in the office with all Bart's old business correspondence – what there was of it," Deborah said, her mind clearly on the extensive plan on her desk. "Cherry will get it out for you. Have a look through that."

Cherry was the highly efficient secretary who in a matter of minutes had produced the file and, for the next half hour, Sam went steadily through the contents.

It was true that his father had been a secretive business-man, much to the detriment of the business after he had disappeared. Very little of his deals had been committed to writing. Maybe he had much to hide. The point was that by this method he had left a chaotic situation behind him, and it had taken all the ingenuity of Deborah and Abel to rebuild the business to which he had obviously thought he would return.

But finally, just at the end of the dusty file of half-completed deals, Sam found what he was looking for.

On a piece of notepaper with a single address in Zurich and a telephone number at the head was the message:

> Dear Mr Sadler,
>   Further to our recent conversation I look forward to seeing you at this address on the date suggested by you to discuss matters of mutual interest.
>   I am,
>   Yours sincerely,
>   Anton Lippe

There it was, as enigmatic and uninformative in his business dealings as Bart was in his. They must have suited each other. It was curious that Bart had kept this document because he had retained little else.

The letter was dated December 1937 and Irene's father had been released in or about the summer of 1938. Sam was disappointed to see that the letter was so old and, dejected, he took it back to the room where Deborah had now been joined by Abel.

"I've found something," he said holding out the faded piece of paper. "It's dated 1937 but it does give an address."

"Sam," Abel looked good-naturedly at the younger man, "why don't you settle down to business with us? There is room for you. There is *need* of you. Your father acknowledged your ability when he made you his heir. We would like to have you working with us, and believe me, business is booming."

Sam shook his head clearly preoccupied with the letter in his hand. "I must go to Zurich just to see if I can find a clue. Besides, I'm too restless, to be honest. I can't settle down to civvy life, much as I hated the army. I'm going to travel. I've made a suggestion to Minnie Fisher that she goes and lives at Upper Park in my absence."

"*Minnie* goes to live at Upper Park?" Deborah raised her head with interest at this potential piece of gossip.

"Of course I shan't be there. I have told her she must use it for as long as she likes."

"Are she and Alexander . . . parting?" Deborah glanced sideways at Abel.

"Minnie finds herself in a very difficult position," Sam replied. "One can understand it. It is very difficult, too, for Alexander."

"Did you talk to Alexander?"

"No. Why should I? If Minnie wants to tell him she can. Anyway she hadn't made up her mind. I thought you might keep an eye on the property while I'm away if anything goes wrong, any repairs need doing. That is, if you don't mind?"

"Sam!" Abel leaned against the desk his arms akimbo. "Are you going to take an interest in the business or not? If not we would like to buy you out."

"For the moment," Sam replied, "I can say nothing. When and if I know what has happened to Bart I'll make a decision. Meanwhile as I have a majority share I shall remain a sleeping partner and hope that you can make me a rich man. If I am to travel and stay in comfortable places I shall have need of all the money I can get."

Later that morning, as he saw Sam out, Abel thought ruefully that it was not for nothing Bart had entrusted his business to his son. Sam was intent on travelling, leaving Deborah and himself to do all the work.

When he returned to the office Deborah was standing by the window watching Sam drive off.

"I shan't be sorry to see my brother go," she said taking Abel's arm. "We'll work much better with him out of the way. He's too restless, a chip off the old block, if you ask me."

"But he gets a large percentage of any profits. That's what I object to. I knew Bart left him very well off. He's as canny as Bart ever was." Abel who had his wife to keep as well as his new establishment spoke feelingly.

"Darling," Deborah put her head against his shoulder, "what does it matter as long as we're happy and have enough? In time Sam might change his mind and we can buy him out. Who knows but that Bart might return?" She looked at him solemnly. "Who knows what the future will bring? We have to live for today. The war has taught us that much."

The house in the prosperous Swiss city of Zurich was in a narrow street that had clearly seen better times. It seemed that some renumbering had been going on and, at first, Sam thought with a sense of despair that he wouldn't be able to locate the exact building where Anton Lippe had lived or, hopefully, still lived even now.

Then beneath the freshly painted numbers he was able to make out the original digits and, finally, he found Number six, the number he had been looking for, quite legible under the newly painted number four.

He stood back and looked up at the house which had long ago been turned into apartments. There was a line of nameplates beside the door. Scrutinising them he could hardly make out any of the names, some had clearly been there a long time.

The door opened quite easily when he pushed it and he found himself in a tiled hall with a stack of unopened mail on the ledge of what had once been a fireplace. In front of him were two doors with nameplates on them and then a flight of uncarpeted stairs.

He looked at the names but they meant nothing to him. Then he began a slow climb to the top. On each landing were two doors, all with a nameplate on the door, none with the name of Lippe.

When he got to the top he felt a sense of despair. There was no sign of Anton Lippe's name, or any way whereby he could possibly find out which apartment he had occupied nine years before.

He stood on the landing at the top of the house and then slowly began to make his way down again. Halfway down a door opened and an elderly woman emerged dressed in a squashed felt hat and a shabby grey coat with a shopping bag over her arm.

She glanced at him cursorily and turned to lock the door.

"Excuse me, madam," Sam said in the halting German he had picked up during the war, "have you lived here for long?"

"*Vous êtes Français?*" The woman peered at him.

"*Anglais,*" Sam said.

"Ah!" The woman nodded and then said in reasonable but heavily accented English, "I thought you looked French. Now, in answer to your question I have lived here since 1925. Why do you ask?"

"Did you ever know a Herr Lippe?"

"Herr Lippe?" The woman gazed at the ceiling as if trying to recall the man in question. "Ah, Herr *Anton* Lippe." She smiled at him triumphantly at this feat of memory. "I used to teach languages and so I have a good memory for names."

187

Sam's heart gave a bound.

"Yes, Anton Lippe. He either lived here or had an office here."

"He lived here," the woman said nodding her head vigorously several times. She pointed her finger upwards. "He lived at the top in a small apartment, like mine. They are all small here."

"Lived?" Sam's heart sank. "He is no longer here?"

"Oh no!" The woman shook her head. "He was a mysterious man. He was taken away, I think by the police. They cleared the whole place, everything, and left the door wide open for all to see. When I went up the following day to try and discover what had caused the upheaval the night before – we all heard it, but no one dared investigate at the time – everything was gone. The place was empty." She made a dramatic gesture with her hand. "Cleaned out."

"Why did they come for him?"

The woman shrugged. "They *say* he was a Jew. The Swiss, you know, didn't like Jews and were in collusion with the Gestapo. Some of them, not all. Money changed hands. They were corrupt like all officials in wartime. I am not really able to say what happened. In those days we didn't ask questions. It was too dangerous for everyone, even here in supposedly neutral Switzerland. Many Jews tried to get in and were refused and some that were here were expelled. Thank God those days are over. I am from Alsace myself. I would like to go back but I don't suppose I ever shall." She looked a little forlorn.

"And you knew nothing more about Herr Lippe?"

"Nothing. When he was here I seldom saw him, occasionally meeting him here on the stairs as today I have met you. He was the sort of person you don't remember. I didn't even know what he did; he was away a lot."

"And when did this happen, this clear out?"

The women studied the floor frowning in an effort to remember.

"In forty-one or forty-two. I can't really remember when,

and I would never have thought about it again if you hadn't reminded me. Was he a relation of yours?"

"No. Nothing to do with me at all. It is just that he might have provided some information I wanted about a relation of mine who also disappeared in the war. It seems he and Herr Lippe knew each other."

"Uh!" The woman shrugged again clearly beginning to lose interest. "There are some things about which we will never know the truth. So many people disappeared, a whole way of life was lost." She gazed at him mournfully. "I'm sorry I was not of more help to you in finding your relative." She looked at his face intently for a moment or two as if committing it to memory, this wizened old woman with bright knowing eyes and unruly wisps of grey hair straggling from under her hat. "There are some mysteries you know that are not meant to be solved. Maybe you were not meant to find Herr Lippe or your relative. Good day to you, sir."

"Good day," Sam said standing aside to let her pass. "You have in fact been very helpful." He was about to offer some notes and then thought better of it. There was a dignity about this former teacher of languages that made him think such a gesture would be resented, however much her circumstances had altered.

He walked slowly out of the building after her and then stood in the road looking up at the top floors wondering which apartment had belonged to Herr Lippe and what sinister events had happened on that night all those years before when he and everything connected with him disappeared.

Sam lit a cigarette, turned up his coat collar against the cold and walked away.

Maybe it was true, he thought, that some mysteries were not meant to be solved.

It was that day in a side street in Zurich, six years after Bart Sadler had disappeared in Berlin, that his son, Sam, finally decided to put out of his mind for good the thought that he would ever see his father again, and start a new life.

189

Fourteen

August 1946

D ora examined the bunch of grapes still ripening on the
vine critically. The *vendange* was still some time off,
but the grapes were very small. They looked undernourished.
Unfortunately, it was the same all along the terraces packed
with vines which had largely gone uncared for during the
war. For the past year she had been trying frantically to
establish the crop, but she had not got Jean's experience
and could no longer call in the help they'd once had from
the trained oenologists who had studied their craft for years.
She knew that very little of this crop would be bought by the
négociants and most of it would have to be thrown away as
it had last year.

It was a depressing business.

She looked down at the river flowing past as timelessly as
it had always done in war and in peace, through good times
and bad. There was something so peaceful about the river. It
seemed to unite her with Jean and his companions who lay
in a quiet cemetery not far away, their graves lovingly tended
by her and the relatives of the men who had died.

Jean was gone, but now, thank God, this area no longer
echoed to the sounds of gunfire. A peace of a sort had
broken out, though Europe seemed as far from recovery as
ever. There was no actual war, but there was no actual peace
either, and the news from further afield seemed like shock
waves spreading outwards. Unrest continued in Palestine,

where the Jews were trying to establish a Jewish state after
the horrors of the Holocaust. There was civil war in China,
insurrection in India, which wished to break with the Empire,
and everywhere a great shortage of food.

Dora felt a hand on her shoulder and turned to see Sally
looking at her.

"Take a break," she suggested. "Let's go and have a cup
of good old-fashioned English tea."

"Why not?" Dora smiled and, tucking her *épinettes* into
the pocket of her apron, put her arm through Sally's as they
strolled back towards the house. There were still a few of the
workers they had had for years tending the vines, but they
were mostly old men now. Many of them had lost sons in
the war; of the ones who remained most preferred work in
the cities to the country. They smiled at her as she passed,
and now and then she stopped for a word of greeting.

"I suppose you've known a lot of them for a long time?"
Sally asked.

"Oh yes, and Jean knew their families all his life. Some
of them he went to school with. Some families have been
coming here for the whole of the century." She sighed. "I
don't know for how much longer."

"What do you mean?" Sally looked at her with concern.

"Well, I have to be realistic. How much longer can I stay
here without an income? We have really no money coming
in and there is a lot of investment needed, to say nothing of
wages."

"Can't the family help?"

"You don't suppose I'd *ask* them? Besides, Mummy
already pays Louise's school fees." Dora looked thoughtful as they came to the back door of the farmhouse and
walked into the dark cool kitchen, thankful to be out of the
sweltering sun.

"You're tired, dear, aren't you?" Sally had gone over to
the sink to fill the kettle as Dora took a seat by the table.

"Sometimes I feel like giving up."

"You can't mean it?"

"I do."

"You mean selling up?"

"Yes, if I can get a buyer, and prices are low."

"And do what? Go where?" Sally put the kettle on the stove and took a chair opposite her friend. Looking at her hand Dora noticed she no longer wore her wedding ring.

"Where's your ring?" she asked.

"I took it off." Sally rubbed her finger as though she had suddenly become self-conscious.

"I see." Dora raised her eyebrows but made no further comment. Her own she wore, and would, for the rest of her life.

"As to where I would go . . ." she leaned back and studied the ceiling, "I don't know. Can't decide. A lot depends on what Louise wants to do." Louise had remained at boarding school in England where she was happy; it gave her continuity.

"Might you go home to your mother?"

"No." Dora shook her head vigorously. "Oh, no. Definitely not. I don't feel English any more, well, not to the extent that I want to live there. Frankly I would rather stay here. Jean is here, close by. I know it sounds sentimental, but I wouldn't like to leave Jean. Who would look after his grave? Then when Louise finishes school will she want to remain in England? I don't know. She's half French and this is her patrimony."

Louise now came for the holidays, sometimes bringing lots of friends who envied her her lovely home and the carefree life she could lead there. For one thing there was no shortage of food.

Sally rose and, the kettle having boiled, made the tea and passed Dora her cup. "Biscuit?" she asked opening a tin.

"Thanks." Dora stretched out her hand, looking at her with affection. "You *are* good."

It was so comfortable here with Sally, so natural, undemanding. It reminded her of the good days with May Williams, the woman she had left Jean for, before their relationship had soured. Even at this late stage in her life she felt as comfortable with women, perhaps more, as she did with men. There was a blurred edge to her sexuality that she had never been able to resolve one way or the other. Now she was convinced it didn't matter. She had been happy with May; in the end she had adored her husband. Now she was beginning to feel the same way about Sally – a woman to whom she had always been attracted. Sally seemed happy too. Moreover she looked bronzed and revitalised, much more relaxed than when she came. She sat down munching her biscuit.

"I have a bit of money," Sally announced. "In fact I have quite a lot. Dad left me and Mum equal shares of his fortune."

"Did he?" Dora studied her biscuit. "I didn't know that."

"Carson knew, of course, but he was very meticulous about touching my money."

"Oh, I know. He was the same with Connie, wouldn't touch a penny. It was because his father was such a spend-thrift, always after women with money."

"The point is," Sally continued, "I do like living here. I love this place and I love the vines. What would you say if I suggested investing in the business, becoming a partner, you know, with you?"

"Do you mean it?" Startled Dora gulped down her tea.

"Yes, I do." Sally stretched out a hand and gazed at her bare finger. "You asked about the ring. Well, I've decided to ask Carson for a divorce. He won't say no. He'll be relieved. And you . . ." she looked nervously across the table, "would you mind? I mean if my living here became permanent?"

Dora rose, and going round the table bent and pressed her cheek against Sally's.

"You know there's nothing I'd like better in the world."

"That's settled then," Sally said shakily. "I'll go and see a lawyer tomorrow."

* * *

23 September 1946   Hotel Ritz
                                                       Madrid

Dear Minnie,

I hope you won't mind a line. I just wondered how
you were getting on. I hope the staff are looking after
you. Do let Deborah or Abel know if you want anything
and please don't pay any bills! They should all be sent to
them anyway. You must know that Dad left me very well
off. Though sometimes devious in his business affairs,
he was careful with money and invested wisely, which
enables me to travel at my leisure and stay in the best
hotels. So please don't think you need to contribute
anything to the upkeep of Upper Park.

Well, I have been to Zurich and discovered that
Anton Lippe, who knew my father, was arrested there
during the war and taken away. I met an old lady who
told me he was supposed to be a Jew! That is very
ironic, because Bart wasn't.

I knew then that my search for my father had ended
and, barring some miracle, I would never see him
again, so I wandered through Europe which, believe
me, is in a pretty parlous state. Parts of Germany,
mostly the cities like Berlin, Dresden, Munich and
Bonn, are flattened. You can't get a hotel room in
Berlin that hasn't had some damage done to it. I
hated Berlin, anyway, and left as soon as I could.
Prague, Budapest, Belgrade are similarly in ruins.
Prices are prohibitive, foodstuff scarce and there are
beggars everywhere.

It is very distressing to think this is what we fought
for. Not for the first time I found myself wondering if
it was all worthwhile.

Spain has been luckier. As you know it remained
neutral during the war, and this is the first decent
hotel I've found for weeks. But there is destruction
from the Civil War and the regime is depressing.
There are pictures of Franco everywhere and a strong

police presence. Opponents of the regime are not tolerated and there are rumours of sudden disappearances
and torture.

I'm going to travel a bit through Spain and then
Portugal. If I can, I'll go across to North Africa,
Morocco and Algeria.

If you would like to write me a line you can get
me poste restante at the following places: Seville
(end September), Lisbon (first two weeks of October), Rabat (end of October), Algiers (beginning of
November).

I'll write again before then. It would be great to hear
from you.

Sam

Carson drew to a halt outside the house where, many years
before, he had first courted Connie, not because he had
wanted to but because his father had insisted that Connie's
fortune would help the family finances.

Carson blushed even now whenever he thought about it.
Connie had been a shy, myopic young woman, awkward and
bashful in his company. Never in his wildest dreams had he
imagined the transformation a few years in Italy would make,
so that when she returned years later to sell her guardian's
house he fell in love with her and this time only persuaded
her with difficulty to be his wife.

Rose Cottage was a pretty house set back from the road
with a wrought-iron fence around it. Opposite was the
rectory whose occupants, and the life within it, had been
so closely bound up with his own family and their fortunes.
He had heard that the rector was nearing retirement and that
he and Sophie were considering moving right out of the
district.

Wenham would never be the same place without them.

Carson put on his hat, got out of the car and strolled up
the path. The house had changed very little since those days:
the same white walls and window frames, the shiny black

painted door with its large, highly polished brass knocker. Walking up the path Carson imagined that even some of the flowers in the garden, now nearing their end, were the same: hollyhocks, foxgloves, fuchsias, dahlias, a brave second showing of delphiniums and lupins.

Connie herself threw open the door just as he was about to knock. She looked rather dishevelled and seemed surprised to see him.

"Carson?"

Carson removed his hat and said with a smile, "Hello. May I come in?"

"Of course." Connie pointed to some baggage in the hall. "I am just packing. Everything is in such a mess."

"Oh!" Carson's smile was replaced by a look of concern. "You're going so soon?"

"Tomorrow. I fly out to Berlin the day after. It's all quite exciting."

Carson didn't reply, but walked through into the sitting room which looked out on to a pretty garden.

"I wish you weren't going," he said turning round.

"But why?" Connie sat down and lit a cigarette.

"Well I just feel like that. I'm sure the refugees can manage without you."

"That's a very selfish attitude, Carson. They need help. Financial too, of course, and I'm giving them quite a bit. I think the Refugee Council is glad of my help on both counts. Don't forget I was a nurse in the fourteen–eighteen war. Netta will join me when she's finished her secretarial course."

"I blame Netta for all this," Carson said grumpily helping himself to a cigarette. "The bloody refugees can get on quite well without the pair of you."

Connie sat looking at him with some amusement.

"You're no longer in control, are you Carson? No longer the leader of the Home Guard. That's your trouble."

"That's a *ridiculous* thing to say." Carson was still cross. The feeling of anticipation, even of euphoria he'd felt since he received the letter from Sally's solicitor had completely evaporated. "There's nothing wrong with a man wanting his family around him after six years of war. Now they're flying off in all directions. I shall be completely on my own."

Toby had just obtained his commission in the army and Leonard was in his first year at King's College, London. Netta was also in London but would be joining her mother in Germany. The birds had flown the nest.

Connie contemplated her one-time husband. How she'd admired him. She, too, was conscious of the association of the house with their early love affair, or rather hers. He hadn't loved her at all. It had been a horrible and humiliating experience. Now the boot was entirely on the other foot. Or, was it?

"Why are you looking at me like that?" Carson asked.

"I'm just thinking, as you probably were, of those days long ago – of the association with this house, a little sad, I guess."

"But it need not be," he said earnestly. "It did have a happy ending and could have again." With the air of an excited schoolboy Carson went and sat beside her producing a letter from his inside breast pocket. "Sally is asking for a divorce."

Connie took the letter from him and slowly read the contents.

"So," she said passing it back. "She wants to live in France. I must say I'm not too surprised."

"You mean about her and Dora . . . ?" Carson failed to finish the sentence.

"Did you ever think she might be . . . ? Connie left the sentence unfinished. Such delicate matters could only be talked about in riddles.

Carson shrugged. "Perhaps. Anyway . . ." he got up, "I just thought I'd let you know that when you come back I'll be free. Perhaps you can think about it in the meantime? You know what I mean?"

"I think I know what you mean, Carson," Connie said also rising and, suddenly, the world seemed a sunnier, more hopeful place again.

"Besides," Carson's tone was gruff, "we owe it to the children."

* * *

11 October 1946   Upper Park
                                                            Wenham
                                                            Dorset

Dear Sam,

What a nice surprise to get your letter. It was very interesting to hear about your travels in Europe, but sad that the recovery is so slow.

I envy you your travels. Part of my desire to join the WAAF was to enable me to travel, and look what happened! Here I am stuck in the country with two small children.

It's not fair to say 'stuck'. I am very happy here and the comfort of Upper Park is a hundred times better than Lally's cottage, sweet though that was. Massie and the babies are most comfortable and the staff very kind and obliging. I am beginning to take an interest in the gardens and Gilbert, the head gardener, is patient with me, and knowledgeable.

Not much happens here. I occasionally see Alexander, but he is busy in London. He has to reorganise the business completely and doesn't come down here as often as he used to. He likes to see the children, but something tells me he is deliberately staying away from me. I can't blame him and I hope he doesn't blame me. We got ourselves into an impossible situation.

Deborah and Abel came over for dinner. I like them. Eliza is very good and comes to see me, and Lally pops over a lot. She misses the children.

That's all for now. Do write again.

With best wishes,
        Minnie

March 1947

Alexander looked out of his office window and watched the boats plying up and down the Thames. It was a grey, gloomy day reflecting his state of mind. He spent most of his time these days in his office, not only because there was a lot of work to do, but because it took his mind off his domestic problems: his increasing isolation from Minnie; his lack of any rapport with Irene to whom he was no closer than when he saw her in the hospital in Germany and found he couldn't even kiss her.

He felt that an iciness had entrapped him in which he no longer felt emotion or even sexual desire. He saw Minnie and their children regularly, but he and she were no longer lovers. Consequently, there was tension and unease between them, unspoken reproaches from Lally and a apparent continued indifference from Irene, as though she didn't care whether she saw him or not.

No wonder he spent most of his time in London buried in his work.

Alexander was in fact very lonely. This wasn't the sort of existence he'd anticipated when he courted and married the exotic Irene, or began a relationship with the beautiful Minnie. He had not been blessed in love, though he had loved and had been loved in return; but fate had not smiled kindly upon him or the women he had loved.

Alexander often walked home through the London streets to spin out his solitary evenings. Occasionally he would stop at his club in St James's for a drink and a meal. Tonight he caught a cab and went straight home. Before he had paid off the driver, Roberts had opened the door looking, for that normally imperturbable servant, slightly agitated.

"Mrs Martyn is in the drawing room, sir," he murmured into Alexander's ear as he took his hat and coat.

"Oh?" Alexander's face brightened and, looking into the hall mirror, he smoothed his hair and checked his tie. "And how is my mother?"

Roberts coughed discreetly and lowered his voice to a whisper, "It is Mrs *Irene* Martyn, sir, your wife."

"Oh!" Alexander felt an even greater depression of the spirits descend on him. Somehow Irene, although she didn't mean to, always presented problems, reinforcing his feelings of guilt.

She was sitting in the drawing room leafing through a magazine, looked up and smiled as he came in.

"I'm so glad to see you," he said, trying not to sound insincere.

"It's my first trip to London. I felt quite adventurous."

"How did you manage?" He sat down opposite her.

"Very well. I took a cab from the station. See," she pointed to either side of her chair. "No stick."

"That's wonderful." Alexander smiled and, getting up, went over to the drinks table. "Sherry, Irene?"

"That would be lovely."

He poured her a dry sherry, a whisky for himself, and handed her her glass.

"Cheers!" he said.

"Cheers, Alexander."

"Continued good health. I mean that sincerely."

"Thank you." She took a sip of her wine. "And thanks to you I have made such a marvellous recovery. You and Lally, and the doctors of course. I can never repay you."

"Nonsense," Alexander said gruffly sitting down again opposite her.

"No honestly. You have been patient, generous and kind."

"I am, after all, your husband," he said pointedly.

"Oh, I know you considered it your duty, but you performed it so generously because you no longer loved me, and that was generous beyond the call of duty."

Alexander studied the shiny tips of his shoes.

"It isn't that I no longer loved you." He looked at her

earnestly. "The situation was complicated."

"I know, by Minnie. I can't blame her. I never did. I certainly don't blame *you*, but sometimes I wished I'd died in Berlin and then you would be free." She leaned forward, her expression grave. "But you see, Alexander, I want you to be free. I want to give you that freedom and offer you a divorce."

"But what will you do?"

"Do what I should have done before, but of course I wasn't strong enough. Now I feel I am. I am going to stay for a few days in London at a hotel and look for a property, somewhere in Kent."

"That's *ridiculous*," he said robustly. "You must stay here. Whatever you say you are not quite well enough. We must keep an eye on you. I . . ." he took another sip of his drink before putting the glass down carefully on the table, "I don't know what to say. I don't know if I want my freedom. You know that things are not the same between Minnie and me."

"But that is my fault. She resents me. She would not be human if she didn't."

"It's not only that . . ." Alexander frowned. "I don't think things can ever be the same. Maybe I should have given more time to Minnie." He passed a hand wearily across his face. "Look, let's go out to dinner. How about the Savoy?" Suddenly excited he looked at his watch. "It's not too late. Remember when we dined there last?"

"How could I forget?" Irene said, suddenly looking shy.

It was the night he had proposed.

That night, in January 1938, they had ordered vintage champagne. He had told her that Bart Sadler had found her father and he would soon be home. She had looked enchanting in a short black velvet evening frock with gold lamé jacket, a single row of pearls round her exquisite neck. A little cheeky pill-box hat had perched saucily forwards on her

201

head, a half-mesh veil obscuring her eyes, those wicked exciting eyes.

They were still the same eyes, only tonight everything else was different. There was no pre-war Krug champagne but a non-vintage bottle of an obscure make.

He wore his business lounge suit and she the grey costume with a white jabot blouse she'd worn up to town. There was no little black hat – no hat at all – no alluring single row of pearls. Opposite him was a war-weary woman who had spent five years being hunted like a rat and whose hair had turned white practically, she'd told him, overnight. But she had never whined or wanted pity. She'd just struggled to get better with the grim determination that had kept her alive during the war.

Now he felt that the white hair gave her a strange beauty and dignity, the eyes still shone with undiminished brilliance and she had resumed her exotic and rather skilful use of make-up: a slash of scarlet lipstick to heighten her colour, yet a more subdued use of rouge and mascara than she'd employed when she was a younger woman.

She looked grave, desirable, even beautiful, and she was still his wife.

Suddenly Alexander longed to take her in his arms, embrace her and comfort her.

He reached out his hand for hers.

"I'm so glad we came," he said as he felt her fingers tightly clasping in his response. "Shall we order?"

Later that night Alexander felt as though he'd started to live again, and next to him Irene smiled into the darkness because she knew that fear and suffering were behind her and that her husband, Alexander, loved her still.

Only they had to get to know each other all over again. It was like starting out afresh.

* * *

23 April 1947   The Hotel Pierre
                                 New York

Dear Minnie

It has been great to get your letters. I think they have all found me, and your latest arrived only this morning. I have been away upstate exploring the country and it has been enough to convince me that America is a wonderful place, vibrant and full of life. Of course, unlike Europe it has been untouched by war. There are no bombed buildings or shattered lives, not that you see, anyway, though millions of Americans fought in the war overseas and there must be plenty around.

I think I might start my own business here. At the moment I'm not sure what that will be.

I'm not very anxious to return to Wenham which was never a very happy place for me. I don't have many good memories of it . . . except meeting you. Like my father when he went abroad before the First War I don't miss it.

But I miss you Minnie. I love your letters. As to the personal news you wrote in your last one, well, it doesn't surprise me that Alexander and Irene have decided to try and make a go of their marriage again. What does surprise me is the generosity with which you have accepted it. You even sound as though you mean it.

But then you are the most generous, good and kind person alive.

Oh, Minnie, I feel you would adore New York.

Is it possible that you might want to join me here, or are you still in love with Alexander?

Sam

September 1947

Carson stood on the platform at Blandford Station waiting with a good deal of impatience for the train to arrive. He

203

paced agitatedly up and down, hands behind his back, a pipe in his mouth.

As the train came in he walked slowly along inspecting the carriages, anxious for some reason that even now Connie might have changed her mind or missed the train.

Then the door of one of the rear coaches opened and she stepped out, turning round to thank someone who was helping her with her bags.

Carson rushed forward to take her luggage and also thanked the man handing them out to her. Then he kissed her on the cheek and, a bag in each hand, led her towards the car.

"It's great to see you," he said glancing down at her. She looked magnificent with her hair swept back and wearing a fashionably long skirt and a short jacket over an open-necked shirt. "You look extremely well. I thought you'd be haggard and emaciated and I'd have to fatten you up."

"Oh, no, we were well fed and looked after. We have to be to be of any use to those we were there to help. Oh, Carson I can't tell you how awful the refugee situation is. There are thousands and thousands of displaced people who have lost their homes and everything."

"Is Netta OK?" he asked anxiously. "Isn't she a bit young for all that?"

"Not at all. Netta is in her element. She organises everybody, just like you." Connie paused and smiled. "She is every bit your daughter, Carson."

Carson put the bags into the boot of the car, saw Connie into her seat and then drove swiftly out of Blandford. Connie, obviously contented to be home, sat back gazing at the familiar countryside through which they were passing.

"I have missed Dorset," she cried. "It's so beautiful, so civilised. They haven't begun to reconstruct Germany, you know. It's an almost impossible task. Berlin is divided between the Russians and the Allies. Some help is desperately needed if the rest of Europe is to survive against the communists. It was a terrible mistake to let the Russians get to Berlin first."

"Don't let's talk about gloomy things," Carson said. "We have enough gloom here. The food crisis is getting even worse. I tell you I am having to turn over every acre we have to fulfil the food quotas. Sometimes I wonder what we went to war for."

"Don't forget it was the same after the last war," Connie said quietly. "We forget. Anyway, tell me all the news, the gossip." She looked at him expectantly. "How's Eliza?"

"She's fine. Oh, and by the way, I have got some surprising news: Minnie and Sam are getting married."

"Minnie and Sam . . ." Connie seemed lost for words. "You mean *our* Sam?"

"Yes." Carson smiled. "Apparently they had a long correspondence while he was away which blossomed into love. She went over to New York to see him, and the news arrived the other day."

"I'm so glad. How lovely. Minnie deserved something good to happen to her," Connie smiled contentedly. "And Alexander?"

"Well, Alexander and Irene are together again, as I think I told you in my last letter. Her health has dramatically improved. What is more Alexander is considering buying Upper Park from Sam who doesn't want to live there any more. Sam and Minnie are to make their home in America."

"How will Lally take that?"

"Oh, quite well. She realises Irene and Alexander want their own home, and they will be near. Irene is expecting."

"That's marvellous news."

"The doctors weren't too thrilled. She will have to take it very easily, but I am very, very happy for them. Even Kate is pleased, but she's spoiled, of course."

"Do you like Irene as much as you liked Minnie?"

"Yes, but in a different way. She's much more mature. She has to be. I guess all the fun was knocked out of her by her experiences. She put no pressure on Alexander, but he clearly cherishes her and that's what matters." Carson studied her profile. "All in all, things have turned out for the best. Don't you agree?"

"Oh, yes." Suddenly Connie became excited. "Oh, *there's* the house. You know I've missed it too. I've been living out of a suitcase. A little stability will be nice."

As Carson stopped the car outside the main door, David ran down the steps, a smile on his face and hurried over to take the bags.

"Welcome home to Pelham's Oak, Lady Woodville," he said.

"*Contessa*, if you please," Carson corrected him woodenly. "Colomb-Paravacini."

"I'm very sorry, sir, madam." David looked abashed.

"However that might soon change." Carson glanced across at Connie who looked away, pretending to ignore his remark. "You may be right after all, who knows?"

After a leisurely tea during which Connie told Carson about the conditions in the refugee camps in Europe and he filled her in on more of local gossip, they went upstairs with her bags. They'd felt very easy and natural with each other from the moment they'd met at the station.

"I've put you in your old room," Carson said opening the door. "I hope you don't mind."

Connie walked across to the window of the room where they'd spent the first night of their marriage. Her heart felt very full as though this was the dawn of a new experience. She was aware of Carson close behind her and, as she reached the window she turned and put her arms around his neck. Simultaneously his encircled her waist.

"I missed you terribly," he said looking into her eyes. "It has been a very long year. Have you thought about what I said before you went away?"

"Yes."

"And the answer?"

"Is yes. Did you ever think it could be anything else?" Her

expression was grave, but there was an impish twinkle in her eyes. "Besides, as you said, we owe it to the children."

When they kissed it felt as if they were first-time lovers, beginning their lives together all over again.

Epilogue

Closing the Circle

August 1950

Almost all the inhabitants of Wenham were in the parish church for the service to mark the departure of Hubert Turner who had been their rector for thirty-seven years. It was also the occasion of the induction of the new rector, the Reverend Duncan Fairbrother who had been an army chaplain in the war. The rectorship of Wenham seemed conducive to longevity. Hubert's father-in-law, the Reverend Austin Lamb, had served the parish for forty years.

Watching her husband process with the new rector to the sanctuary, Sophie, whose own life was so bound up with this small town in the Blackmore Vale, recalled that day in August 1913 when a very similar ceremony had been enacted. It had also been a beautiful day then and the future had seemed promising, as they could not hear the distant rumble of war.

This time war was behind them, though the world was still an uneasy place and no one slept too soundly in their beds while the great powers hurled abuse and issued threats against one another.

In 1913 they had dedicated a window in memory of Sophie's first husband, George Woodville, who had died of fever in New Guinea. Today the sun, as it had then, shone through the window and caught the exact angle of the cross casting its shadow over those portrayed beneath it.

Thirty-seven years. It seemed a lifetime, full of memories,

211

good and bad. But, since deciding to move north to Hubert's beloved Lake District, where they'd bought a house, Sophie had many times regretted that decision. After all she was Wenham born and bred and, except for the years in New Guinea, had lived there all her life.

She turned to look at her friend Eliza, sitting next to her, who gave her a sympathetic smile. Eliza, always a support whatever the occasion, and now in her eighty-ninth year, was also born and bred in Wenham and had never left it.

Eliza's memories on this milestone day went back a very long way, were just as full as Sophie's, just as profound and, in many ways, just as sad.

The window dedicated to Sophie's husband, George, who had also been her nephew was also dedicated to the memory of her son Laurence. Laurence and George, for ever etched in glass, were the figures looking up at the cross, their hands eternally clasped in prayer. In their way they had achieved immortality; no one would forget them. Would that everyone close to her could have a similar memorial. Her first husband, Ryder, was buried in the family vault together with Laurence, her brother Guy, his wives Margaret and Agnes, and all the family who had passed away. One day, inevitably, she would join them. Rather than frightening it was, strangely, a comforting thought.

Eliza squeezed the arm of her old, old friend; they exchanged glances. She thought of all the people who had been alive in 1913 and were dead now, of the cruel fates that had overtaken members of her family including Laurence's widow Sarah-Jane who had been murdered by a man who had never been found; her son-in-law Jean who had been shot in the war. Dora standing beside her had her share of deprivation and suffering, Connie had been cut off from everyone for the duration of the war. Yet, by a strange irony, good had come out of it too. Carson and Connie had been joined together again in marriage, and Alexander's wife Irene had been miraculously restored to him after six dreadful years. Alexander's daughter Kate stood between them in the pew behind her. Their baby, Reuben, was at home with his nurse. On Alexander's other side was Lally, also a beloved friend, now aged ninety yet able to hold her own with the younger generation.

Eliza glanced round at the family, their voices raised in the processional hymn 'He who would valiant be'. As the two priests knelt in front of the altar and began the bidding prayers, Carson stepped forward to read the first lesson. Carson, who had the living of Wenham in his gift, had chosen a soldier as the new rector, a young man who had been awarded, like him, the Military Cross for gallantry.

Carson's children as well as Connie were all in the church: Toby in military uniform, following in a tradition close to his father's heart; Leonard a new graduate; Netta on leave from Germany. Deborah stood next to her mother, Sophie. As far away as possible her sister Ruth had slipped into a side aisle, clasping her prayer book in her hands, her eyes fixed on the pulpit. She had decided to move north to help look after her parents and shake the dust of Wenham from her feet. She had refused to let Abel have a divorce and she and Deborah never communicated with each other. Their eyes never met in church and probably never would again. For this reason Abel had stayed away. How sad it was when families fell out.

Sally, too, had remained in France to look after the vines – those precious vines. Sam and Minnie, together with Minnie's children, had made their home in America.

Sophie, who had always been troubled by scruples, felt that in many ways she had been a bad mother, not intentionally of course, but her children had had difficult lives. Only Tim, her son by Hubert, standing on her right side had managed to lead, so far, an uncomplicated life and, to the joy of his parents, was studying for Holy Orders.

Halfway down the church were Elizabeth, Carson's half-sister, and her husband, Graham Temple. Their family had all turned out well, despite early poverty. Their sons, Robert and Tom, were studying to follow their father into the law. Their daughter Betsy had married a local, prosperous farmer and Jack Sprogett had been a hero in the war, an act which had revitalised his life. Only Mary, Alexander's first wife, was no longer with them. On the way into the church they had laid flowers on her grave.

As the bidding prayers came to an end Carson, an impressive figure, tall, resolute, aristocratic, a true *paterfamilias* if ever there was one, slowly mounted the pulpit. Looking at him fondly, his aunt Eliza thought it was difficult to believe he had once been a feckless youth who had caused his parents so much grief, from whom no village maiden was said to be safe.

After glancing around as though he was in charge of the ceremonies he put on a pair of reading spectacles and cleared his throat before announcing in a clear tone, "The lesson is taken from the book of Ecclesiasticus, chapter 44, verses one to fourteen: Let us all praise famous men, and our fathers that begat us . . ."

Sophie listened, absorbed, as he read on, a text so well known to her. How apposite all the words were, applying both to men and women. There were people rich in virtue, born of those who had left a name behind them. There were some to whom there was no memorial, who perished as if they had never been . . .

She thought of Bart, who had once been her lover. He was Sam's father. Somehow his fate had been the most cruel and, though she tried not to think of him, he hadn't deserved it. He had disappeared, it seemed for ever. For the first time for many years she tried to force herself to think good of Bart, and said a little prayer for him in her heart. After all was this not a time for forgiveness, for a sense of joy and the hope of peace?

"Their bodies are buried in peace," Carson concluded in resonant tones, "and their name unto generation and generation. Let the people show forth their wisdom and the church declare their praise."

Carson closed the massive Bible, a gift to the church from a much earlier Woodville, and slowly looked round at the people crammed into every nook and cranny of the church. The rear doors were open and he could see the crowd pressing forward, straining to hear every word. The sun streamed through the stained-glass windows.

His heart was very full. It seemed a good day to be alive.

"I just want to say a few words," he said, "on this day that we say farewell to one rector and welcome another. It is a day for looking backwards as well as forwards.

"All of you here have experienced many things since Hubert Turner was installed the year before the First World War began.

"A few years ago we finished another war. Let us pray that, during the time of the new rector, history will not repeat itself. I want to thank Hubert and wish him and Sophie well in their new life. I want to welcome Duncan Fairbrother who served all during the last war comforting many. I know he will be a worthy successor to Hubert and maybe, who knows, he might see the people of this parish through to the millennium, fifty years hence."

There was a rustle of amusement at this notion while Carson fondly surveyed the congregation below him. They were his people, young and old. He and his family were one with them, inextricably linked. Their welfare was his; his and his children's theirs. So it had been for hundreds of years and so, he was sure, would it continue.

Afterwards, the congregation streamed out into the sun, pausing to chat and greet one another, to shake the hand of the new rector and that of the one who was about to depart. Hubert's handkerchief was never very far away from his eyes and he and Sophie clutched each other for mutual support.

Finally they were led away by Carson and Connie, and the rest of the family got into their cars and drove off. Then, as on so many momentous occasions in the past, the body of the congregation, having closed their shops and locked their houses, climbed into or on to various forms of transport – cars, carts, horses even a tractor or two – or made their way on foot, along the winding road to the home of the Woodvilles.

It was, after all, at Pelham's Oak that, by tradition, the citizens of Wenham foregathered to mark the various milestones affecting the life of the town or that of the family, whether in war or peace, good times or bad, fair weather or foul, sadness or celebration.

So it always had been and so, as long as there were Woodvilles left alive, it always would.